The Taming of a Shrew: A Retelling

David Bruce

Published by David Bruce, 2022.

THE TAMING OF A SHREW: A RETELLING

First edition. July 19, 2022.

Copyright © 2022 David Bruce.

ISBN: 979-8201470494

Written by David Bruce.

Table of Contents

Dedication

Dedicated to My Uncle Reuben Saturday

When he was a young man, my mother's brother Reuben wanted to escape from poverty and lard sandwiches, so he tried to run away from it. He stole a car so he could drive up north where he hoped to find opportunity, but he got caught and ended up on a Georgia chain gang for several months. In a chain gang, prisoners are shackled every few feet by the ankles to a long length of chain to keep them from escaping. They work in the hot sun while shackled to the chain, and when they sleep, they are shackled to the bed. No freedom, hard work, hot sun, no pay, bad food, and some mean guards.

When my uncle got released from the chain gang, he hitchhiked up north. He did what a lot of people trying to escape from poverty do: He drifted. He drifted from town to town, seeking opportunity and not finding it. He worked when he could, but the jobs were temporary and low pay. My uncle slept rough often, and he was hungry often. Once, when he was completely broke and completely hungry, he saw a restaurant with a buffet and went inside and asked to speak to the manager. He said, "I am very hungry, I don't have any money, and I would appreciate it very much if you would give me any food that the restaurant is going to throw away. I will be happy to wait by the rear entrance until you are ready to throw away food."

The manager told him to sit down at a table, and then the manager went to the buffet, loaded a big plate high with food, and gave it to him free of charge.

One way out of poverty is to get a good job, and my uncle got out of poverty by getting a job working with sheet metal.

My uncle's work ethic helped him. His employer sent him to California to do some special sheet-metal work, and the people in California wanted to keep him there. They explained that their

California employees liked to come to work late, leave early, and take many days off. It was difficult to get someone who would show up and do the work they were supposed to do and were paid to do.

My uncle was also good with money. He got married, bought a house, and raised six children. Each time he made a mortgage payment, he paid extra money so he could pay off the mortgage faster.

If there was a sale on food, he bought lots of it. For example, if there was a sale on peanut butter, two jars for the price of one, he would buy twelve jars and sometimes go back the next day and buy six more jars.

If you went in his pantry — a closet set aside to store food — you saw that it was packed with food. If you went in his kitchen, you saw that he had taken off the doors of the high cabinets in which he stored food so that he could see the food. If you went in his bedroom, you saw that he had all the regular bedroom furniture, but he also had lots of shelves he had installed. The shelves were loaded with things that he had bought on sale that he knew his family could use: food (of course), light bulbs, toothpaste, toilet paper, etc. His bedroom looked like a warehouse.

Once he made a bad purchase: he bought a case of baked beans. Beans are beans, but the sauce they came in can taste good or bad, and the sauce these beans came in tasted bad. His kids told him, "Dad, throw those beans away! They're awful!"

But when you grow up poor, you don't throw beans away. For a long time, whenever my uncle and his family ate baked beans, they ate a mixture of one can of good baked beans and one can of bad baked beans.

My uncle's kids never had to eat lard sandwiches.

Educate Yourself
Read Like A Wolf Eats
Be Excellent to Each Other
Books Then, Books Now, Books Forever

***

In this retelling, as in all my retellings, I have tried to make the work of literature accessible to modern readers who may lack some of the knowledge about mythology, religion, and history that the literary work's contemporary audience had.

Do you know a language other than English? If you do, I give you permission to translate this book, copyright your translation, publish or self-publish it, and keep all the royalties for yourself. (Do give me credit, of course, for the original retelling.)

I would like to see my retellings of classic literature used in schools, so I give permission to the country of Finland (and all other countries) to give copies of this book to all students forever. I also give permission to the state of Texas (and all other states) to give copies of this book to all students forever. I also give permission to all teachers to give copies of this book to all students forever.

Teachers need not actually teach my retellings. Teachers are welcome to give students copies of my eBooks as background material. For example, if they are teaching Homer's *Iliad* and *Odyssey*, teachers are welcome to give students copies of my *Virgil's* Aeneid: *A Retelling in Prose* and tell students, "Here's another ancient epic you may want to read in your spare time."

CAST OF CHARACTERS

In The Introduction:

Sly, A Drunkard.
A Bartender.
A Lord (who calls himself in jest "Simon," aka "Sim").
Tom, a Serving-man to the Lord.
Will, a Serving-man to the Lord.
Sander, an Actor.
Tom, an Actor.
A Boy, an Actor.
A Messenger.
Serving-men, Huntsmen.

***

In The Play:

Jerobel, Duke of Sestos.
Aurelius, His Son.
Valeria, Servant (male) to Aurelius.
Polidor, a Gentleman of Athens.
A Boy, Servant to Polidor.
Ferando, a Gentleman of Athens.
Sander, Servant to Ferando.
Tom, Servant to Ferando.
Will, Servant to Ferando.
Alfonso, a Rich Citizen of Athens.
Kate, Eldest Daughter to Alfonso.
Philema, Middle Daughter to Alfonso.
Emelia, Youngest Daughter to Alfonso.
Phylotus, a Merchant of Athens.
A Tailor.

***

NOTES:

Peter Lukacs has an excellent annotated text of the play at ElizabethanDrama.org. It can be downloaded free:

<https://tinyurl.com/y6clafkk>.

Also available there is a free theater script of the play.

His arrangement of the play is copyrighted: © arrangement copyright Peter Lukacs and ElizabethanDrama.org, 2020.

Peter Lukacs writes: "This play is in the public domain, and this script may be freely copied and distributed."

He also writes, "The text of the play is taken from Frederick Boas' edition of *The Taming of a Shrew* of 1908, but with much original wording and spelling reinstated from the quarto of 1594."

Earliest Extant Edition: 1594

The Taming of a Shrew may be a parody of Christopher Marlowe's writing by someone other than Marlowe, or it may be written by Marlowe himself as a parody of himself. Lukacs writes:

> Scholar Donna N. Murphy, in her book *The Marlowe-Shakespeare Continuum* (Cambridge: Cambridge Scholars Publishing, 2015), argues that the author of *A Shrew* is in fact **Christopher Marlowe**, who wrote the play to be performed for his sister's wedding in 1590. While I do not propose to rehearse any of Murphy's reasoning here, I will suggest that there is some evidence (some of it based on my own research) to support the theory that Marlowe in fact wrote *A Shrew* to parody himself.

In this society, a good wife is an obedient wife.

— A Good Wife —

The Elizabethans regarded a good wife as an obedient wife. Here are some Bible passages (Saint James Bible) on wives, husbands, and marriages.

A wife's duty to her husband:

"Wives, submit yourselves unto your own husbands, as unto the Lord." — Ephesians 5:22

"For the husband is the head of the wife, even as Christ is the head of the church: and he is the savior of the body." — Ephesians 5:23

"Therefore as the church is subject unto Christ, so let the wives be [that is, submit] to their own husbands in everything." — Ephesians 5:24

A husband's duty to his wife:

"Husbands, love your wives, even as Christ also loved the church, and gave himself for it;" — Ephesians 5:25

"Likewise, you husbands, dwell with them according to knowledge, giving honor to the wife, as to the weaker vessel, and as being heirs together of the grace of life; that your prayers be not hindered." — 1 Peter 3:7

"But if any provide not for his own, and especially for those of his own house, he has denied the faith, and is worse than an infidel." — 1 Timothy 5:8

What husbands and wives should do:

"Nevertheless let everyone of you in particular so love his wife even as himself; and the wife see that she reverence her husband." — Ephesians 5:33

INTRODUCTION

A bartender appeared at the front door of a country alehouse, shoving a very drunk man named Sly out of his alehouse.

The bartender said, "You son of a whore! You drunken slave! You had best be gone and vomit and empty your drunken stomach somewhere else, for in this alehouse you shall not rest tonight."

Sly was apparently so drunk that he had been vomiting.

The bartender went back into the alehouse.

Wandering away a short distance from the alehouse, Sly drunkenly said, "Pish posh, by Jeez, bartender, I'll beat you soon!

"Fill up for us another drinking vessel, and all's paid for!

"Look, I drink it of my own instigation."

By "instigation," he meant "initiative."

Recalling the Latin for "All's well," Sly added, "*Omne bene*: Here I'll lie awhile.

"Why, bartender, I say, fill up for us a fresh tankard here!

"Heigh-ho, here's good warm lying."

He fell asleep on the ground, which would have been cold instead of warm to him if he were not drunk.

A Nobleman — that is, a Lord — and his huntsmen were returning to their home after hunting.

The well-educated Lord said in poetic language that they were returning home because of the arrival of dark night:

"Now that the gloomy shadow of the night,

"Longing to view Orion's drizzling looks,

"Leaps from the Antarctic world to the sky,

"And dims the sky with her pitch-black breath,

"And dark night shades over the crystal heavens,

"Here break we off our hunting for tonight."

When the constellation Orion appears in England in late autumn, it is often accompanied by stormy weather, and so the Lord referred to "Orion's drizzling looks."

The Lord continued, "Leash the hounds in pairs and let us hurry home, and tell the huntsmen to see that the hounds are well fed, for they have all deserved it well today."

Seeing the sleeping, drunken Sly, the Lord said, "But wait, what sleepy fellow is this who is lying here? Or is he dead instead of asleep?

"One of you see what he needs."

One of the serving-men examined Sly and said, "My Lord, this is nothing but a drunken sleep; his head is too heavy for his body and so he cannot hold it up, and he has drunk so much that he can go no further."

The Lord said, "Bah, how the slavish villain stinks of drink!"

He called to Sly, "Ho, Sirrah, arise! What! So sound asleep?"

People such as Lords could call men of lower class "Sirrah."

Thinking of playing a practical joke on the drunken Sly, the Lord then ordered his serving-men, "Go, pick him up and carry him to my house, and carry him easily for fear he will wake up.

"In my fairest chamber make a fire, and set a sumptuous banquet on the table, and put my richest clothing on his back. Then set him at the table in a chair.

"When this is done, in anticipation for when he shall awake, let heavenly music play about him always."

This culture lacked radio and television and YouTube, but rich people such as the Lord paid musicians and kept them on standby to play live for him.

The Lord added, "Two of you carry him away from here, and then I'II tell you what practical joke I have devised, but see in any case that you don't wake him."

Two serving-men carried away Sly.

Later, at his house, the Lord said to his serving-men, "Now take my cloak and give me one of yours."

He put it on and said, "We are all equal fellows now, we are all serving-men, and see that you treat me like a serving-man, for we will wait upon and serve this drunken man in order to see his face when he awakens and finds himself dressed in such expensive attire, with heavenly music sounding in his ears, and such a banquet set before his eyes that the fellow surely will think he is in Heaven.

"But we will be around him when he awakens. See that you call him 'Lord' every chance you get.

He said to the servant named Will, "You offer him his horse to ride."

He said to the servant named Tom, "And you offer him his hawks and hounds to hunt the deer."

The Lord then said, "And I will ask what suits he means to wear.

"Whatever he says, see that you do not laugh, but always behave in such a way that will convince him that he is a Lord."

A messenger arrived and said, "If it please your honor, your actors have come, and they await your honor's pleasure here."

This society had traveling troupes of actors who journeyed through the countryside and performed at the homes of the wealthy.

The Lord said, "This is the best and fittest time they could have chosen to come here. Tell one or two of them to come here immediately.

"Now I will fit myself accordingly and pretend to be a servant to the drunken man, for the actors shall perform a play for him when he awakes."

Three actors arrived: Sander and Tom (two adult men carrying packs on their backs), and a boy. In this society, women and girls did not act. Boys performed female roles.

The Lord asked, "Now, sirs, what kind of plays do you have?"

Sander said, "Indeed, my Lord, you may have a tragical, or a comodity, or whatever you will."

Sanders used words mistakenly: "tragical" for "tragedy," and "comodity" for "comedy."

Tom, who knew more about words than Sander, said, "A comedy, you should say. By God's wounds, you shame us all."

The Lord asked, "And what's the name of your comedy?"

Sander replied, "Indeed, my Lord, it is called *The Taming of a Shrew*. It is a good lesson for us, my Lord, for us who are married men."

The Lord said, "*The Taming of a Shrew*: That's excellent, to be sure. Go and see that you get ready to perform immediately, for you must play before a Lord tonight. Say that you are his men and that I am your fellow. He's somewhat foolish, but whatever he says, see that you are not dashed out of countenance, but continue to treat him as a Lord."

To the boy-actor, he said, "And, Sirrah, go make yourself ready immediately, and dress yourself like some lovely lady, and when I call, see that you come to me, for I will say to him that you are his wife.

"Flirt with him and hug him in your arms, and if he wants to go to bed with you, make up some excuse and say you will soon but not now.

"Be gone, I say, and see that you act the part of his wife well!"

"Fear not, my Lord," the boy-actor said, "I'll flirt with him and tease him well enough, and I will make him think I love him mightily."

The boy-actor exited.

The Lord then said to Sander and Tom, "Now, sirs, go and make yourselves ready, too, for you must perform the play as soon as he wakes up.

"Oh, this is excellent," Sander said. "Sirrah Tom, we must play before a foolish Lord. Come, let's go make ourselves ready. Go and get a dishcloth to clean your shoes, and I'll take care of the stage props."

He then turned toward the Lord and said, "My Lord, we must have a shoulder of mutton for a stage prop, and a little vinegar to make our devil roar."

No devil appears in the play — unless Kate the shrew and Ferando the tamer are metaphorical devils. Apparently, Sander was arranging for food to feed the troupe of actors.

"Very well," the Lord said.

He ordered a serving-man, "Sirrah, see that they lack nothing."

— Scene 2 —

In a room in the Lord's house, Sly, who was now richly dressed, slept in a chair placed in front of a table on which two servants had placed good, expensive food.

The first servant expressed satisfaction at a job well done: "So."

He then said to the second servant, "Sirrah, now go and call my Lord, and tell him that all things are ready as he wished."

The second servant replied, "Set some wine upon the board, and then I'll go and fetch my Lord immediately."

The first servant placed wine on the table, and then the second servant exited.

The Lord and his serving-men entered the room.

"How are things now!" the Lord said. "Are all things ready?"

"Aye, my Lord," the first servant answered.

"Then sound the music, and I'll wake the drunken man immediately," the Lord said, "and see that you do as previously I gave you the order."

He said loudly to Sly, "My Lord, my Lord!"

Sly continued to snore, and the Lord said to his serving-men, "He sleeps soundly."

He said loudly again, "My Lord!"

Waking, and continuing to think that he was in the inn, Sly said, "Bartender, give us a little small ale. Heigh-ho!"

"Small ale" is weak ale.

"Heigh-ho" is an expression that indicates weariness.

"Here's wine, my Lord, the purest blood of the grape," the Lord said.

"For which Lord?" Sly asked.

The Lord replied, "For your honor, my Lord."

"Who, I?" Sly asked. "Am I a Lord?"

He looked at the clothes he was wearing and said, "Jesus! What fine apparel I have got on!"

The Lord said, "Your honor has more clothing much richer by far to wear, and if it would please you, I will fetch better clothing immediately."

The serving-man named Will said, "And if your honor would please to go horseback riding, I'll fetch you lusty steeds that are swifter of pace than the winged horse Pegasus in all his pride, which ran so swiftly over the Persian plains."

The serving-man named Tom said, "And if your honor would please to hunt the deer, your hounds stand ready leashed in pairs at the door. These hounds in running will overtake the deer and make the tiger, which runs fast and far, broken-winded."

"By the mass, I think I am a Lord indeed," Sly said.

He then asked the Lord, who was dressed as a serving-man, "What's your name?"

"Simon, if it please your honor," the Lord answered.

Sly said, "Simon — that's as much to say 'Simion' or 'Sim.'"

These were two nicknames for "Simon."

He ordered the Lord, "Put forth your hand and fill my drinking vessel," and then he said, "Give me your hand, Sim. Am I a Lord indeed?"

"Aye, my gracious Lord," the Lord said, "and your lovely wife has for a long time mourned for your absence here."

Soon the boy-actor would say that Sly had been mentally ill and not in his right mind.

The Lord said about Sly's "wife," "Now with joy behold where she is coming here in order to express her joy over your honor's safe return."

The boy-actor, now wearing woman's clothing, entered the room.

"Sim, is this she?" Sly asked.

The Lord answered, "Aye, my Lord."

"By the Mass!" Sly said. "She's a pretty girl! What's her name?"

The boy-actor said, "Oh, that my lovely Lord would once give me the favor of looking at me, and stop having these frantic, insane fits. Or if I were now but eloquent enough to paint in words what I'll perform in deeds, I know your honor then would pity me."

"Hark you, mistress, will you eat a piece of bread?" Sly asked.

People in Sly's social class ate much bread. Much richer fare was on the table, but Sly was not accustomed to eating or offering to others such fare.

He then said, "Come sit down on my knee."

The boy-actor sat on Sly's knee.

Sly then ordered, "Sim, drink to her, Sim, for she and I will go to bed soon."

The Lord said, "May it please you, your honor's actors have come to offer your honor a play."

"A play, Sim?" Sly said. "Oh, splendid! They are *my* players?"

Some Lords were wealthy enough to hire an entire company of actors to live on the Lord's estate and perform plays when the Lord requested.

The Lord answered, "Aye, my Lord."

"Isn't there a fool in the play?" Sly asked, hoping that the answer would be, *Yes, there is a comic character in the play.*

The Lord answered, "Yes, there is, my Lord."

"When will they play, Sim?" Sly asked.

"Whenever it pleases your honor, they are ready," the Lord said.

The boy-actor said, "My Lord, I'll go and tell them to begin their play."

"Do, but make sure that you come back again," Sly said.

The boy-actor replied, "I promise you, my Lord, I will not abandon you like that."

The boy-actor exited.

"Come, Sim, where are the actors?" Sly said. "Sim, stand by me, and we'll heckle the actors out of their coats."

The Lord said, "I'll call them, my Lord."

He then called, "Ho! Where are you there?"

CHAPTER 1

— 1.1 —

In Athens on the street in front of Alfonso's house, two young gentlemen, Aurelius and Polidor, and their servants, Valeria and a boy, met.

Polidor was a resident of Athens and Aurelius was his newly arrived friend. Valeria was Aurelius' serving-man, and the boy-servant served Polidor. Aurelius was the son of Jerobel, Duke of Sestos.

Polidor greeted Aurelius, "Welcome to Athens, my beloved friend! Welcome to Plato's schools and Aristotle's walks."

Plato and Aristotle were two famous ancient Greek philosophers. Plato had been the pupil of Socrates, and Aristotle tutored the young Alexander the Great.

Aurelius had come to Athens to study philosophy.

Polidor continued, "Welcome from Sestos, famous for the love of good Leander and his tragedy, for whom the Hellespont weeps brinish tears."

Sestos was located on the European shore of the Hellespont, the narrow strait between the Sea of Marmara and the Aegean Sea. In mythology, a woman named Hero, who lived in Sestos, loved a man named Leander, who lived on the Asian side of the strait. Each night, Leander would swim across the Hellespont, guided by the light of a lamp that Hero lit. One night the wind blew out the lamp, and Leander drowned. After discovering his body, Hero committed suicide in order to be with him.

Polidor continued, "The greatest grief is I cannot give the entertainment I wish I could to my dearest friend."

Aurelius replied, "Thanks, noble Polidor, my second self and best friend. The faithful love that I have found in you has made me leave the princely court of my father — the Duke of Sestos' three-times-renowned seat — to come to Athens thus to find and visit

13

you, which since I have so happily done, my fortune now I account as great as formerly did Caesar when he was most successful at warfare.

"But tell me, noble friend, where shall we lodge, for I am unacquainted in and with this place," Polidor replied.

"My Lord, if you are willing to partake of scholar's fare, my house, myself, and all is yours to use," Polidor said. "You and your men shall stay and lodge with me."

Many scholars are impoverished, and so their food and lodgings are poor.

"With all my heart I will repay your kindness," Aurelius said.

Alfonso and his three daughters came out of their house.

Kate was Alfonso's eldest daughter.

Philema was Alfonso's middle daughter.

Emelia was Alfonso's youngest daughter.

Seeing them, Aurelius said, "But wait a moment. What dames are these so light-skinned and bright of hue, whose eyes are brighter than the lamps — the stars — of heaven, fairer than pearls and precious jewels, far more lovely than is the morning Sun when first she opens her oriental gates and rises in the East?"

In this society, lighter complexions were regarded as more beautiful than darker complexions.

Alfonso said, "Daughters, leave now and hurry to the church, and I will hurry down to the quay to see what merchandise has come ashore."

A quay is a wharf.

Alfonso and his three daughters exited.

Polidor said to his best friend, "Why, how are you now, my Lord? What! Depressed to see these damsels leave so soon?"

"Trust me, my friend," Aurelius said. "I must confess to you that I took so much delight in these fair dames that I wish they had not gone so soon.

"If you can, tell me who they are, and who is the old man who went with them, for I long to see them once again."

"I cannot blame your honor, my good Lord," Polidor said, "for the three ladies are lovely, wise, beautiful, and young.

"And, sweet friend, one of them, the youngest of the three, I long have loved and she has long loved me. But we could never find a way to achieve our desired joys."

Such desired joys can be achieved through marriage.

"Why, isn't her father willing to agree to the marriage match?" Aurelius asked.

"Yes, trust me," Polidor said. "But he has solemnly sworn that his eldest daughter shall first be married before he grants his younger daughters permission to love.

"Therefore, the men who intend to get the loves of the two younger daughters must first provide for the eldest daughter if they will find success in love.

"But he who marries the eldest daughter shall be so fettered that it will be as if he were wedded to the devil himself, for such a scold as the eldest daughter never did live.

"And until the eldest daughter is married, none of the other daughters will be allowed to marry, which makes me think that all my labor spent pursuing the youngest daughter is lost.

"But whoever can get the eldest daughter's firm good will shall be sure to have a large dowry, for her father is a man of mighty wealth and an ancient citizen of the town, and he was the old man who went along with the three dames."

Aurelius said, "But in my opinion he shall keep the eldest daughter always because she is unlikely to marry. And yet I must love his second daughter, who is the image of honor and nobility and in whose sweet person is comprised the sum of nature's skill and heavenly majesty."

Polidor said, "I like your choice, and I am glad you didn't choose my choice.

"If you wish to pursue your love, we must devise a plan and find someone who will attempt to wed this devilish scold — and I know the man."

Taking action immediately, he ordered his servant, "Come here, boy, and listen. Make your way, Sirrah, to Ferando's house. Ask him to take the pains to come to me, for I must speak with him immediately."

"I will, sir," the boy servant said, "and I will fetch him here quickly."

The boy servant exited.

"Ferando is a man, I think, who will fit the eldest daughter's temperament well," Polidor said. "He is as blunt in speech as she is sharp of tongue, and he, I think, will match her in every way. And yet he is a man of sufficient wealth, and as for his person he is worth as good as she.

"If he wins her to be his wife, then we both may freely visit our loves."

Aurelius said, "Oh, I wish I could see the center of my soul, the dame whose sacred beauty has enchanted me. She is more beautiful than was the Grecian Helen of Troy for whose sweet sake so many princes died, who came with a thousand ships to Tenedos!"

In his tragedy *Doctor Faustus*, Christopher Marlowe referred to the beautiful Helen of Troy as possessing "the face which launched a thousand ships." Homer's *Iliad* recounts some of the events near the end of the Trojan War, a ten-year war that started after Paris, a prince of Troy, ran off with Helen, the wife of Menelaus, the King of Sparta.

Tenedos is an island near Troy.

Aurelius continued, "But when we come into her father's house, tell him I am a son of a merchant of Sestos, and I have come on business here to Athens."

Continuing with his plan to wed Alfonso's second daughter, Aurelius ordered Valeria, his serving-man, "Sirrah, I will exchange clothing with you here at this time. Now you will pretend to be the

Duke of Sestos' son. Revel and enjoy yourself and spend my money as if you were myself, for I will court my love in this disguise."

Aurelius would pretend to be a serving-man, while Valeria would pretend to be Aurelius.

Valeria objected, "My Lord, what if the Duke, your father, would by some means come to Athens in order to see how you are profiting in these public schools of philosophy? And what if he would find me clothed thus in your attire? How do you think he would take it then, my Lord?"

"Tush, fear not, Valeria, leave it to me," Aurelius said. "But wait, here comes some other company."

Ferando and his serving-man Sander entered the scene. Sander was wearing the typical attire of a serving-man in this society: a blue coat. Servants' attire — livery — differed to show which master the servant served.

Polidor said, "Here comes the man whom I told you about."

Ferando was Polidor's choice to pursue Kate, Alfonso's shrewish daughter.

"Good morning, gentlemen, to both of you!" Ferando said. "How are you now, Polidor? What, man, are you still in love? Forever wooing and never succeeding? May God send me better luck when I shall woo."

Sander said to Ferando, "I promise you success, master, if you take my advice."

"Why, Sirrah, are you so cunning?" Ferando said.

"Who, I? It would be better for you by five marks, if you could tell how to do it as well as I," Sander said.

Marks were 16th century English money. This strange "Athens" used English money such as crowns, and some of the citizens' names were more Italian than Greek.

Polidor said to Sander, "I wish that your master were in the mood to test himself and see how he could woo a wench."

The word "wench" at this time was often used affectionately.

"Indeed, I am even now going to woo a woman," Ferando said.

Sander backed up that statement: "Indeed, sir, my master's going about this business right now."

"Where will you woo, indeed, Ferando?" Polidor asked. "Tell me the truth."

Ferando said, "I am going to woo Signor Alfonso's eldest daughter, bonny Kate, the most patient wench alive." He was sarcastic when he referred to "bonny Kate, the most patient wench alive," as was shown by his next statement: "The devil himself scarcely dares to venture to woo her."

"Signor" is an Italian courtesy title; it can also be spelled "Signior."

He continued, "Signor Alfonso has promised me six thousand crowns if I can win her to be my wife."

This was a very good dowry.

Ferando added, "She and I must woo with scolding, surely, and I will make her scold until she is exhausted and can argue against me no longer, or else give up and agree to marry me."

"How do you like this, Aurelius?" Polidor said. "I think he knew what was in our minds before we sent to him."

He then asked Ferando, "But tell me, when do you mean to speak with her?"

"Indeed, immediately," Ferando said. "Just stand to the side, out of the way, and I will make her father bring her here, and she, and I, and he, will talk alone, privately."

"We will do that with all our hearts!" Polidor said. "Come, Aurelius, let us go, and leave him here alone."

Aurelius and Polonius exited.

Ferando called, "Ho! Signor Alfonso, who's within there?"

Alfonso returned from the quay and said, "Signor Ferando, you're welcome heartily. You are a stranger, sir, to my house."

Either this was the first time that Ferando had been to Alfonso's house, or he had not been there for a while.

Alfonso continued, "Listen, sir. Look, I'll do what I promised you, if you get my daughter's love."

Ferando replied, "Then after I have talked a word or two with her, you step in and give her hand to me, and tell her when the marriage day shall be. For I know she would willingly be married. And when our nuptial rites have once been performed, let me alone to tame her well enough.

"Now call her forth so that I may speak with her."

Alfonso called for her, and Kate arrived on the scene.

"Ha, Kate!" Alfonso said. "Come hither, wench, and listen to me. Treat this gentleman as friendly as you can."

Alfonso exited. Ferando's serving-man Sander stood behind a door to give some privacy to Ferando and Kate, but he was still within hearing distance. A good servant knows more about his master than the master usually thinks the servant knows.

"Twenty good mornings to my lovely Kate!" Ferando said.

"You jest, I am sure. Is she yours already?" Kate said.

"I tell you, Kate, I know you love me well," Ferando said.

"The devil you do!" Kate said. "Who told you that?"

"My mind, sweet Kate, does say that I am the man who must wed and bed and marry bonny Kate," Ferando said.

"Was ever seen so gross an ass as this?" Kate said.

"Aye, to stand so long and never get a kiss," Ferando said.

Ferando attempted to kiss Kate, but failed.

"Hands off, I say, and get away from this place," Kate said, "or I will set my ten commandments in your face."

Kate's ten commandments were her fingers: She was threatening to scratch Ferando's face, thereby commanding him to leave her alone.

"I pray that you do, Kate," Ferando said. "They say you are a shrew, and I like you the better for it, for I would have you so."

He wanted a wife with spirit — but one who would respect and obey him.

"Let go of my hand for fear it will reach your ear and hit you," Kate said.

"No, Kate, this hand is mine, and I am your love," Ferando said.

"Indeed, sir, no," Kate said. "The woodcock lacks his tail."

Woodcocks were notoriously stupid birds that were easily trapped.

The tail could be a body part that men have and women do not have.

"But yet his bill — his mouth — will serve, if the other fail," Ferando said.

He kissed her.

Alfonso re-entered the scene.

"How are things now, Ferando?" Alfonso asked. "What says my daughter?"

"She's willing to marry me, sir," Ferando said, "and she loves me as she loves her life."

"It is for the sake of your skin then, but not to be your wife," Kate said.

She may have meant that she wanted to scratch his skin.

"Come here, Kate, and let me give your hand to him whom I have chosen for your love," Alfonso said, "and you tomorrow — Sunday — shall be wed to him."

"Why, father, what do you mean to do with me," Kate said. "To give me thus to this brain-sick madman, who in his mood doesn't care if he murders me?"

She thought, *But yet I will consent and marry him, for I think that I have lived too long a maiden, and I will match him and be his equal, too, or else his manhood's good.*

Only a strong, capable man could tame Kate.

"Give me your hand," Alfonso replied. "Ferando loves you well, and he will with wealth and ease maintain your high and stately quality of life."

He then said, "Here, Ferando, take her for your wife, and Sunday — tomorrow — shall be your wedding day."

Ferando said, "Why, didn't I tell you I should be the man?"

Now that Ferando and Alfonso were to be son-in-law and father-in-law, they began to call each other "Son" and "Father."

Ferando said, "Father, I leave my lovely Kate with you. Prepare yourselves for our marriage day, for I must hurry to my country house, to see that provision may be made to entertain my Kate when she comes."

Alfonso said, "Do so.

"Come, Kate, why do you look so sad? Be merry, wench, your wedding day's at hand.

"Son, fare you well, and see that you keep your promise."

Alfonso didn't want Ferando to reconsider his decision to marry Kate. He didn't want his eldest daughter to be abandoned at the altar.

Alfonso and Kate exited.

"So," Ferando said. "All, thus far, goes well."

He called, "Ho, Sander!"

Sander came out from behind the door where he had been standing to give Alfonso and the others some privacy.

Laughing, he said, in part to himself, "Sander, indeed, you're a beast. I cry to God heartily for mercy — my heart's ready to run out of my belly with laughing. I stood behind the door all this while and heard what you said to her."

"Why, did you think that I did not speak well to her?" Ferando asked.

Sander said, "You spoke like an ass to her. I'll tell you what, if I had been there to have wooed her, and if I had this cloak on that you have and if I had been in your shoes, I would have had her before she had gone a step further.

"But you talk of woodcocks with her, and I cannot tell you what else."

Tails can be embarrassing to speak about.

"Well, Sirrah," Ferando said, "and yet you see I have got her for all this. She will be my bride."

"Aye, by the Virgin Mary, it was more by good luck than by any good cunning. I hope she'll make you one of the head-men of the parish shortly."

The kind of "head-man" Sander may have meant may have been a man with horns on his head — in other words, a cuckold.

"Well, Sirrah, leave your jesting and go to Polidor's house," Ferando said. "Find there the young gentleman who was here with me, and tell him the details of all you know. Tell him that on this Sunday Kate and I must be married. And if he asks you where I have gone, tell him into the country to my house, and I'll be here again Sunday."

Ferando exited.

Alone, Sander said, "I assure you, master, fear not that I will not do my business."

Ferando was about to marry into one of the richest families in Athens. He would have a notable rise in status, and as his servant, Sander would also have a notable rise in status.

Sander continued, "Now hang him who has not a livery coat to slash it out and swash it out and swagger it out among the proudest of them."

One can slash with a sword, and one can swash by making a noise with a sword. A swashbuckler is a person who beats a shield of the kind called a buckler with a sword. Such a person can be a *miles gloriosus*, which is Latin for a swaggering, boastful soldier. In the theater, such soldiers are stock comic characters.

He continued, "Why, look you now, I'll scarcely put up with plain 'Sander' now at any of their hands, for if anybody wants to have anything to do with my master, immediately they will come crouching and bowing to me to say, 'I beg you, good *Master* Sander, speak a good word for me,' and they will beg me to arrange an appointment for him.

Then I will be very stout and arrogant and stand upon my dignity and behave pompously to an extraordinary degree.

"Why, I have a life like a giant now, except that my master lately has such a pestilent mind that he will marry a shrewish woman now. I have a pretty wench who is my sister, and I had thought to have recommended my master to her; their marriage would have been a good deal in my way to make me rise higher in society, but now he's engaged to another woman already."

Polidor's boy-servant entered the scene.

He greeted Sander, "Friend, well met!"

Thinking about his soon-to-be rise in status, Sander was affronted by the informal greeting and said, "By God's wounds, 'Friend, well met!'

"I bet my life he doesn't see my master's livery — the coat I am wearing. If he did, he would treat me with more respect."

He then greeted Polidor's boy-servant, "Plain friend hop-of-my-thumb, do you know who we are?"

He was using the majestic plural because he regarded himself as vastly superior to this small boy.

"Trust me, sir, it is the custom where I was born to salute men after this manner," Polidor's boy-servant said. "Yet, notwithstanding, if you are angry at me for calling you 'friend,' I am the more sorry for it, hoping the name of a fool will make you amends for all."

Sander thought that the boy-servant was calling himself a fool, but the boy-servant was calling Sander a fool.

Sander thought, *The slave is sorry for his fault; now we cannot be angry.*

He then asked, "Well, what's the business that you have with us."

"By the Virgin Mary, sir," the boy-servant said, "I hear you are employed by Signor Ferando."

"Aye, and if you are not blind, you may see," Sander said. "*Ecce signum*, here."

He pointed to his livery, which showed that he was employed by Signor Ferando.

Ecce signum is Latin for "Behold the sign."

The boy-servant asked, "Shall I entreat you to deliver for me a message to your master?"

"Aye, you may," Sander said, "if you tell us from where you come."

"By the Virgin Mary, sir, I serve young Polidor, your master's friend," the boy-servant said.

"Do you serve him, and what's your name?" Sander asked.

"My name, Sirrah, I tell you, Sirrah, is called Catapie," the boy-servant said.

"Cake and pie?" Sander said. "Oh, my teeth waters to have a piece of you."

"Why, slave, would you eat me?" the boy-servant asked.

"Eat you?" Sander said. "Who would not eat cake and pie?"

"Why, villain, my name is Catapie," the boy-servant said. "But will you tell me where your master is?"

"No, you must first tell me where your master is, for I have good news for him, I can tell you," Sander said.

"Why, see there where he comes," the boy-servant said, pointing.

Polidor, Aurelius, and Valeria entered the scene. Polidor was the boy-servant's master.

"Come, sweet Aurelius, my faithful friend," Polidor said. "Now we will go to see those lovely dames, richer in beauty than the orient pearl, whiter than is the Alpine crystal mould, and far more lovely than the Terean plant, which blushing in the air turns to a stone."

Polidor's being in love was making him speak poetically. The Alpine crystal mould was the icy top of an Alp. (The word "mould" literally means "top of the head.") The Terean plant was Mediterranean coral. In this society, people believed that coral was a sea-plant that turned to stone and turned reddish when exposed to air.

Seeing Sander and the boy-servant, Polidor asked, "Sander, what is the news with you?"

"By the Virgin Mary, sir," Sander said, "my master sends you word that you must come to his wedding tomorrow."

"What!" Polidor said. "Shall he be married then?"

"Indeed, yes," Sander said. "You think he stands as long about getting married as you do?"

"Where has your master gone now?" Polidor asked.

"By the Virgin Mary," Sander said, "he's gone to our house in the country in order to make all things ready in preparation for when my new mistress comes there, but he'll come again tomorrow."

"This is suddenly dispatched, it seems," Polidor said.

He then ordered, "Well, Sirrah boy-servant, take Sander in with you, and take him to the pantry immediately and give him some refreshments."

"I will, sir," the boy-servant replied. "Come, Sander."

Sander and the boy-servant exited.

Aurelius had made a change in his plan to court Alfonso's second daughter: Philema. Previously, the plan was for Valeria to impersonate Aurelius. Now Aurelius had decided that Valeria would impersonate a music tutor.

Aurelius said to his servant, "Valeria, as formerly we did plan, take your lute and go to Alfonso's house, and say that Polidor sent you there."

Polidor said, "Aye, Valeria, for he spoke to me and asked me to help him find some skillful musician to teach his eldest daughter, Kate, to play on the lute. And you, I know, will fit his turn and serve his purpose so well that you shall get great favor at his hands.

"Go, Valeria, and say I sent you to him."

"I will, sir," Valeria said, "and I will await your coming at Alfonso's house."

Valeria exited.

Polidor said, "Now, sweet Aurelius, through this plan we shall have the opportunity to court our loves, for while Kate is learning on the lute, her sisters may take the opportunity to steal abroad and go outside, for otherwise she'll keep them both within the house and make them work while she herself plays.

"But come, let's go to Alfonso's house, and see how Valeria and Kate agree. I doubt his music will please his scholar."

It is difficult to please a shrew.

"But wait," Polidor said. "Here comes Alfonso."

Alfonso walked over to them and said, "Master Polidor, you are well met. I thank you for the man you sent to me. I think he is a good musician. I have set my daughter and him together."

Looking at Aurelius, Alfonso asked, "But is this gentleman a friend of yours?"

"He is," Polidor said, "Please, sir, welcome him. He's the son of a wealthy merchant of Sestos."

Alfonso said to Aurelius, "You're welcome, sir, and if my house can provide you with anything that may content your mind, I ask you, sir, to make bold with me and request it."

"I thank you, sir," Aurelius replied, "and if what I have got, by merchandise or travel on the seas, satins, or fine linen, or azure-colored silk, or precious fiery-pointed gems of India, you shall command both them, myself, and all."

Azure is blue.

"Thanks, gentle sir," Alfonso replied.

He then said, "Polidor, take him in, and bid him welcome, too, to my house, for you, I think, must be my second son."

Because Ferando was marrying Kate, Polidor would be able to marry Alfonso's third daughter: Emelia. Thus, Polidor would be Alfonso's second son-in-law.

Alfonso continued, "Polidor, don't you know? Ferando must marry Kate, and tomorrow is the day of the wedding."

"Such news I heard," Polidor said, "and I came here now to confirm it."

"Polidor, it is true," Alfonso said. "Go, and let me alone now, for I must see to the preparations for when the bridegroom comes so that all things will be as he wishes, and so I'll leave you for an hour or two."

Alfonso exited.

Polidor said, "Come then, Aurelius, come in with me, and we'll go and sit awhile and chat with Alfonso's middle and youngest daughters, and afterward bring them forth to go for a stroll and take the air.

Polidor and Aurelius exited.

Sly, who had been drinking and watching the play, asked, "Sim, when will the fool come again?"

Sander is the fool.

The real Lord replied, "He'll come again, my Lord, soon."

"Give us some more drink here," Sly said. "By God's wounds, where's the bartender?"

Sly, still drunk and confused, thought he was at the inn.

He then said, "Here, Sim, eat some of these things," referring to the food on the table.

"So I do, my Lord," the real Lord replied.

"Here, Sim, I drink to you," Sly said.

"My Lord, here come the actors again," the real Lord said.

"Oh, splendid," Sly said. "Here's two fine gentlewomen!"

Actually the characters were Kate and Aurelius' man-servant Valeria, who was wearing tutor's clothing that Sly apparently thought was feminine attire.

CHAPTER 2

— 2.1 —

In a room in Alfonso's house were Valeria, who was holding a lute, and Kate.

Valeria said to himself about the power of music, "The senseless trees by music have been moved, and at the sound of pleasant tuned strings, savage beasts have hung down their listening heads, as though they had been cast into a trance. So then it may be that she — Kate the shrew — whom nothing can please, with music's sound in time may be surprised."

One kind of surprise is a military ambush.

He then said to Kate, "Come, lovely mistress, will you take your lute, and play the lesson that I most recently taught you?"

"It does not matter whether I do or not," Kate said, "for, believe me, I take no great delight in it."

"I wish, sweet mistress, that it lay in me to help you to that thing that's your delight," Valeria said.

A thing can be a penis.

If Kate does not like music, perhaps she likes sex.

"In you?" Kate said. "With a pestilence, are you so kind? Then make a night-cap of your fiddle's case to warm your head and hide your filthy face."

Kate was using the word "kind" sarcastically.

In this society, a case can be a sheath, or a vagina. And a head can be part of a penis.

"If that, sweet mistress, were your heart's content," Valeria said, "you should command a greater thing than that, although it were ten times to my disgrace."

One meaning of Valeria's comment is that he would do a greater task than the one she had asked him, even if it resulted in him being embarrassed ten times as much as doing the first task.

In the second meaning, "a greater thing" is "a bigger penis."

"You're so kind," Kate said. "It would be a pity if you would be hanged — and yet I think the fool looks at me from the corners of his eyes."

In this society, looking at someone this way was an indication of jealous love.

"Why, mistress, do you mock me?" Valeria asked.

"No, but I mean to move you," Kate said.

Kate being Kate, she wanted to move Valeria to anger.

Valeria being Valeria, he wanted to move his penis in and out of Kate.

"Well, will you play a little?" Valeria asked.

No doubt he wanted to play a little in bed.

"Aye, give me the lute," Kate said.

She played.

"That note was false," Valeria said. "Play it again."

"Then you mend it," Kate said. "You play it, you filthy ass!"

Valeria, pretending to mishear Kate, said, "What! Do you command me to kiss your arse?"

"How is it now, Jack Sauce? You're a jolly mate," Kate said. "You had best be still, lest I hit your head and make your music fly about your ears. I'll make it and your foolish coxcomb meet."

The word "coxcomb" referred to the top of his head.

Kate attempted to make Valeria's music and coxcomb meet by hitting him on the head with his lute.

"Stop, mistress," Valeria said. "By God's wounds, will you break my lute?"

"Aye, on your head, if you speak to me."

She threw the lute down and said, "There, pick it up, and fiddle somewhere else. And see that you come no more into this place, lest I clap your fiddle on your face."

Kate stormed out of the room.

"By God's wounds, shall I teach her to play upon the lute?" Valeria said. "The devil shall teach her first. I am glad she's gone, for I was never so afraid in all my life that my lute would fly about my ears.

"My master shall teach her himself as far as I'm concerned, for I'll keep myself far enough outside her reach.

"He and Polidor sent me before themselves to be with her and teach her to play the lute while they courted the other gentlewomen, and here I think they come together."

Aurelius and Philema entered the scene, as did Polidor and Emelia.

"How are you now, Valeria? Where's Kate, your mistress?" Polidor asked.

"Out for vengeance, I think, and nowhere else," Valeria said.

"Why, Valeria, will she not learn easily to play the lute?" Aurelius asked.

"Yes, by our lady, the Virgin Mary, she has learnt too much already," Valeria said. "And I would have felt more blows from her, had I not spoken to her kindly. But she shall never receive lessons from me again."

"Well, Valeria," Aurelius said, "go to my chamber, and keep company with someone who came today from Sestos, where my aged father dwells."

Valeria exited.

"Come, fair Emelia, my lovely love," Polidor said. "You are brighter than the polished palace of the Sun, the eyesight of the glorious firmament, in whose bright looks sparkles the radiant fire wily Prometheus slyly stole from Jove, infusing breath, life, motion, soul, to every object stricken by your eyes!"

Prometheus was a Titan — the Titans were giants in ancient Greek mythology — who was sympathetic to humans and stole fire from Jove, aka Jupiter, King of gods and humans, to give to them.

Polidor continued, "Oh, fair Emelia, I pine for you, and I either must enjoy your love, or die."

"Bah, man, I know you will not die for love," Emelia said. "Ah, Polidor, you need not grieve. Eternal Heaven will sooner be dissolved and melted, and all that pierces Phoebe's silver eye, before such an occurrence as me rejecting you befalls to Polidor."

"Thanks, fair Emelia, for these sweet words," Polidor replied.

He turned to Philema and asked, "But what does Philema say to her friend?"

In this society, a friend can be a lover.

"Why, I am buying merchandise from him," Philema said.

Aurelius was pretending to be a merchant.

He said to Philema, "Mistress, you shall not need to buy from me, for when I crossed the bubbling Canibey and sailed along the crystal Hellespont, I filled my coffers with the spoils of wealthy mines, where I caused millions of laboring Moors to excavate the caverns of the earth, to seek for strange and newfound precious stones and dive into the sea to gather pearl as fair as Juno offered Priam's son."

In the famous Judgment of Paris, Paris, who was King Priam's son and so a prince of Troy, judged a beauty contest whose contestants were three goddesses: Juno, Venus, and Minerva. Each goddess offered Paris a bribe if he would choose her as winner. Juno offered him command over cities that would bring him vast wealth. Minerva offered him prowess in battle. Paris choose Venus, who had offered him the most beautiful woman in the world: Helen, who became Helen of Troy.

Aurelius then said to Philema, "And you shall take your free and liberal choice of all."

Philema replied, "I thank you, sir, and I wish that Philema might in any courtesy repay you so, as she with willing heart could well bestow!"

Alfonso entered the scene.

"How are you now, daughters?" he asked. "Has Ferando come?"

"Not yet, father," Emelia said. "I wonder that he stays away so long."

The day was Sunday, the day of Ferando's wedding to Kate.

"And where's your sister Kate?" Alfonso asked. "Why is she is not here?"

"She is getting ready, father, to go to church," Philema said, "in case Ferando were to come."

"I promise you that he'll not be long away," Polidor said.

"Go inside, daughters, and tell your sister to prepare herself for our arrival," Alfonso said. "And see that you go to church along with us."

Philema and Emelia exited.

"I marvel that Ferando has not arrived," Alfonso said.

"His tailor, perhaps, has been too slow in readying the apparel that Ferando means to wear at his wedding," Polidor said, "for there is no question but Ferando is determined to wear today some fantastic suits that are richly powdered with precious stones, spotted with liquid gold, and thickly set with pearl. Such clothing he intends shall be his wedding suit."

"I would not care — I wouldn't — what cost he did bestow on gold or silk to make his wedding suit," Alfonso said, "as long as he himself were here, for I had rather lose a thousand crowns than he should deceive us here today and desert Kate at the altar — but wait, I think I see him coming."

Ferando arrived, but he was basely attired, and he wore a red cap on his head.

In this society, people of the lower classes wore red caps.

Ferando, who was not a member of the lower classes, was not dressed in the fancy wedding clothing others expected him to be wearing.

"Good morning, father," Ferando said to Alfonso.

He then said, "Polidor, we are well met.

"You wonder, I know, that I have stayed away so long and been so long in coming."

"Aye, by the Virgin Mary, son, we were almost convinced that we would scarcely have had our bridegroom here," Alfonso said. "But tell us why you are thus so basely attired."

"Thus so richly, father, you should have said," Ferando replied. "For when my wife and I are married, she's such a shrew, if we should once fall out, she'll pull my costly suits of clothing over my ears. Therefore, I am thus attired for a while.

"For I tell you that many things are in my head, and none must know thereof but Kate and me, for we shall live like lambs and lions, to be sure.

"Lambs to lions never were so tame, if once they lie within the lion's paws, as Kate to me once we are married."

Ferando expected to be the lion, and Kate to be the lamb, in their marriage — once he had tamed her.

He continued, "Therefore come, let us go to church immediately."

"Bah, Ferando — not thus attired, for shame!" Polidor said. "Come to my house and there dress yourself in one of the twenty suits of clothing that I have never worn."

"Tush, Polidor," Ferando said, "I have as many fantastic suits made to fit my desires as any in Athens and as richly made as was the massive robe that recently adorned the stately ambassador of the Persian King, and I have chosen to wear this suit from them."

The word "fantastic" can mean "elaborate" or "grotesque."

"I beg of you, Ferando, let me entreat you, before you go to the church with us, to put some other suit of clothing on your back," Alfonso pleaded.

"Not for the world, if I might gain it by doing so," Ferando replied. "And therefore take me like this, or not at all."

Kate entered the scene.

"But wait, see where my Kate is coming!" Ferando said. "I must greet her — how fares my lovely Kate? Are you ready? Shall we go to church?"

"Not I," Kate said. "Not with one so mad and so basely attired. I will not marry such a filthy, slavish groom, who, as it seems, sometimes is out of his mind, or else he would not thus have come to us."

A groom can be a bridegroom or a lowly servant.

"Tush, Kate, these words add greater love in me, and they make me think you more beautiful than before," Ferando said. "Sweet Kate, you are lovelier than the purple robe of Diana, the goddess of the hunt, and you are whiter than are the snowy Apennine mountains or the icy hair that grows on the chin of Boreas, god of the North Wind!

Ferando continued, "Father, I swear by Ibis' golden beak, more fair and radiant is my bonny Kate than is the silver Xanthus when it embraces the ruddy Simoïs at the feet of Mount Ida."

Ibis is an Egyptian sacred bird.

The Xanthus and Simoïs are Trojan rivers. The Simoïs is here called ruddy — reddish — because during the Trojan War the Greek warrior Achilles killed many, many Trojans and threw their bodies into it.

Mount Ida is a mountain near Troy.

Ferando continued, "And don't care, sweet Kate, about how I am clad. You shall have garments made of Median silk, inlaid with precious jewels fetched from far by Italian merchants who with Russian prows plow huge furrows in the Mediterranean Sea, and better far my lovely Kate shall wear.

"So then come, sweet love, and let us go to the church, for this I swear shall be my wedding suit."

Kate exited.

"Come, gentlemen, go along with us," Alfonso said. "For clothed like this, do what we can, Ferando will be wed."

They exited.

— 2.2 —

Polidor's boy-servant and Sander talked together in a room in Alfonso's house.

"Come hither, Sirrah boy," the boy-servant said.

Sander, a grown man, was insulted.

"Boy, oh, disgrace to my person! By God's wounds! 'Boy'! In your face! You have many 'boys' with such pickadevants — beards like mine — I am sure! By God's wounds, shouldn't you have a bloody nose for this?"

"Come, come, I was only joking," the boy-servant said. "Where is that piece of pie that I gave you to keep?"

"The pie?" Sander said. "Aye, your mind is more on your belly than to go and see what your master is doing."

"Tush, it doesn't matter, man," the boy-servant said. "I ask you to give the piece of pie to me; I am very hungry, I promise you."

"Why, you may take it, and the devil burst you with it!" Sander said. "One cannot save a bit after supper but you are always ready to munch it up."

"Why come, man," the boy-servant said. "We shall have good food and drink soon at the bride-house, for your master's gone to church to be married already, and there's such food and drink as surpasses anything."

"Oh, splendid," Sander said. "I wish I had eaten no food this week, for I have not a corner left in my belly to put a venison meat pie in. I think I shall burst myself with eating, for I'll so cram down the tarts and the marzipans, to an extent beyond belief."

"Aye," the boy-servant said, "but how will you fare now your master's married? Your mistress is such a devil that she'll quickly make you forget to eat because she'll beat you so."

"Let my master handle that, for he'll make her tame well enough before long, I promise you," Sander said, "for he's grown to be such a churl now that he beats me excessively, even over the smallest thing.

"But in my opinion, Sirrah, Alfonso's youngest daughter is a very pretty wench, and if I thought your master would not have her, I'd have a fling at her myself. I'll see soon whether it will be a match or not; if it will not, I'll try hard to win her for myself, I promise you."

"By God's wounds, you slave," the boy-servant said, "will you be a rival with my master in his love? Speak but one more such word, and I'll cut off one of your legs."

"Oh, cruel judicial sentence!" Sander said. "Nay, then, Sirrah, my tongue shall talk no more to you. By the Virgin Mary, the walking stick I am holding shall tell the trusty message of his master — me — on your forehead, you abusious villain; therefore, prepare yourself."

By "abusious," Sander meant "abusive."

"Come here, you imperfectious slave," the boy-servant said.

By "imperfectious," the boy-servant meant "imperfect."

He continued, "Because of your beggary and poverty, here, there's two shillings for you to pay for the healing of your left leg, which I intend furiously to invade, or to maim at the least."

"Oh, supernodical fool!" Sander said.

By "supernodical," Sander meant "very silly." The word "noddy" means "fool."

He continued, "Well, I'll take your two shillings, but I'll bar striking at legs."

"I won't, for I'll strike anywhere," the boy-servant said.

"Here, here, take your two shillings again," Sander said. "I'll see you hanged before I'll fight with you. I got a broken shin the other day. It is not healed yet, and therefore I'll not fight. Come, come, why should we fall out?"

"Well, Sirrah, your fair words have somewhat lessened my anger," the boy-servant said. "I am content for this once to put it up and be friends with you. But wait, see where they all are coming from the church. It's likely they are married already."

Ferando and Kate, Alfonso, Polidor and Emelia, and Aurelius and Philema entered the scene.

"Father, farewell!" Ferando said to Alfonso. "My Kate and I must go home."

He ordered Sander, his servant, "Sirrah, go and make ready my horse immediately."

"Your horse?" Alfonso said. "What, Son, I hope you are only joking! I am sure you will not go so suddenly."

"Let him go or tarry," Kate said. "I am resolved to stay and not to travel on my wedding-day."

"Tut, Kate, I tell you we must go home," Ferando said.

He then said to Sander, who was not doing his duty, "Villain, have you saddled my horse?"

"Which horse?" Sander said. "Your curtal?"

A curtal is a horse with a cropped tail.

"By God's wounds, you slave," Ferando said. "Do you stand babbling here? Saddle the bay gelding for your mistress."

A gelding is a castrated horse. A bay horse is a reddish-brown horse.

"Don't saddle it for me," Kate said, "for I'll not go."

"The hostler will not let me have him," Sander said. "You owe ten-pence for his food, and sixpence for stuffing my mistress' saddle."

Saddles of the time were stuffed with such materials as wool, hay, and straw.

"Here, villain, go and pay the hostler right away," Ferando said, giving Sander the money needed.

"Shall I give them another peck of lavender?" Sander asked.

"Out, slave, and bring them immediately to the door!" Ferando thundered.

"Why, son, I hope at least you'll dine with us!" Alfonso said.

"Please, master, let's stay until dinner is over," Sander pleaded.

"By God's wounds," Ferando thundered, "villain, are you still here?"

Sander exited.

"Come, Kate, our dinner will be provided at home," Ferando said.

"But not for me," Kate said, "for here I mean to dine. I'll have my will in this as well as you. Though you in a mad mood would leave your friends, despite you, I'll tarry with them still."

"Aye, Kate, so you shall, but at some other time," Ferando said. "When your sisters here shall be married, then you and I will keep our wedding-day in better fashion than now we can provide. For here I promise you before them all, we will before long return to them again.

"Come, Kate, don't stand on terms; we will go away. This is my day; tomorrow you shall rule, and I will do whatever you command.

"Gentlemen, farewell; we'll take our leave. It will be late before we arrive home."

Ferando and Kate exited.

"Farewell, Ferando, since you insist on leaving!" Polidor said.

"So mad a couple I never did see," Alfonso said.

"They're even as well-matched as I would wish," Emelia said.

"And yet I hardly think that he can tame her," Philema said, "for when he is done, she will do whatever she wishes."

"Her manhood then is good, I do believe," Aurelius said.

"Aurelius, unless I miss my mark, her tongue will walk if she holds her hands," Polidor said.

He believed that even if Kate holds her hands and does not beat her husband, her tongue will metaphorically walk all over him.

Polidor continued, "I fear that before half a month passes, he'll curse the priest who married him so quickly. And yet it may be she will be reclaimed, for she has grown very patient of late."

"May God hold that it may continue still!" Alfonso said. "I would be loath that they should disagree, but he, I hope, will rule her after a while."

"Within the next two days, I will ride to him and see how lovingly they agree and get along," Polidor said.

"Now, Aurelius, what do you say to this?" Alfonso said. "Have you sent to Sestos, as you said you would, to inform your father of your love? For I would gladly learn that he approves of it, and if he is the man you tell me he is, I guess he is a merchant of great wealth and I have seen him often at Athens here, and for his sake I assure you that you are welcome."

Polidor said, "And so you are welcome to me, while Polidor lives."

"I find it so, right worthy gentlemen," Aurelius said. "And of what worth I value your friendship, I leave to you to decide for yourself.

"But as for the requital and repayment of your past favors to me, which so far remain unpaid, I vow that it shall be remembered and repaid to the full.

"As for my father's coming to this place, I expect him within this week at the most."

"Enough, Aurelius!" Alfonso said. "But we forget our marriage dinner, now the bride is gone. Let us see what food they left behind."

CHAPTER 3

— 3.1 —

Sander and two or three serving-men talked together in a room in Ferando's house.

"Come, sirs," Sander said, "provide all things as fast as you can, for my master's nearby and my new mistress and all, and he sent me before him to see that all things would be ready for his arrival."

"Welcome home, Sander!" Tom, a serving-man, said. "Sirrah, how does our new mistress look? They say she's a plaguey, vexatious shrew."

"Aye, she is," Sander said, "and that you shall find, I can tell you, if you don't please her well. Why, my master has such extraordinary trouble with her, and he himself is like a madman."

"Why, Sander, what does he say?" Will, another serving-man, asked.

"Why, I'll tell you what," Sander said. "When they went to church to be married, he put on an old jacket and a pair of canvas breeches that went down to the small of his leg just above the ankle and a red cap on his head, and he looked so comic that you will burst yourself with laughing when you see him. He's dressed even as good as a fool as far as I'm concerned."

Fashionable breeches — pants — of the time reached only to the knees. Canvas was an inexpensive material worn by the lower classes; a person of Ferando's social status would be expected to wear expensive material such as velvet.

Sander continued, "And then, when they were going to dinner, he made me saddle the horse, and away he came, and never stayed for dinner, and therefore you had best get supper ready for when they come, for they are nearby, I am sure, by this time."

"By God's wounds," Tom said. "See! They have come already."

Ferando and Kate entered the scene.

"Now welcome, Kate!" Ferando said.

He shouted for the serving-men, "Where's these villains?

"Here! What! Supper is not yet upon the table, nor has the table been set! Nothing has been done at all?

"Where's that villain that I sent before me?"

"Now, *adsum*, sir," Sander said, using the Latin word for "I am here."

"Come here, you villain," Ferando said. "I'll cut off your nose, you rogue! Help me off with my boots."

To the other servants, he said with mock-courtesy, "Will it please you to lay the tablecloth on the table?"

He yelled about Sander, "By God's wounds, the villain hurts my foot!"

Then he ordered him, "Pull easily, I say!"

He yelled, "Yet again he hurts my foot!"

He then stood up and beat all his servants.

The serving-men got busy and covered the table with the tablecloth and brought in the food.

Ferando looked at the food and yelled, "By God's wounds! Burnt and scorched! Who made this food?"

Will said, "Indeed, John the cook."

Ferando threw down the table and food and all, and he beat the serving-men.

"Go, you villains!" Ferando yelled. "Bring me such food? Out of my sight, I say, and carry the food away!

"Come, Kate, we'll have other food provided."

He then asked Sander, "Is there a fire in my chamber, sir?"

"Aye, indeed," Sander said.

Ferando and Kate exited.

The serving-men ate all the food.

"By God's wounds," Tom said, "I think, on my conscience, that my master's become a madman since he was married."

"I laughed at what a blow he gave Sander for pulling off his boots," Will said.

Unseen, Ferando entered the room again.

"I hurt his foot on purpose, man," Sander said, unaware that his master could hear him.

"Did you, indeed, you damned villain?" Ferando said.

He beat all his serving-men and made them flee the room.

He then addressed you, the readers of this book:

"This irritable mood I must hold awhile in order to bridle and restrain my headstrong wife with curbs of hunger, lack of ease, and want of sleep. Neither sleep nor food shall she enjoy tonight.

"I'll mew her up as men do mew their hawks: I'll lock her in her room as men lock up hawks in their cages. And I'll make her gently come to the lure of food as hawks are taught to come."

The lure was a long cord at the end of which were attached meat and feathers (added to make the meat look like a small bird).

Ferando continued, "Even if she were as stubborn or as full of strength as were the Thracian horses Alcides — Hercules — tamed, the horses that King Egeus fed with the flesh of men, yet would I pull her down and make her come as hungry hawks fly to their lure in order to feed."

Actually, it was King Diomedes who owned the human-flesh-eating horses Hercules was required to bring to King Eurystheus in one of his famous labors. King Aegeus owned the Augean stables that Hercules had to clean in another of his famous labors.

— 3.2 —

Aurelius and his servant, Valeria, talked together on a street in Athens.

"Valeria, listen carefully," Aurelius said. "I have a lovely love, as bright as is the crystalline heaven, as fair as is the Milky Way of Jove, as chaste as Phoebe — aka Diana, virgin goddess of the hunt — in her summer sports, as soft and tender as the azure — bluish — down that encircles Cytherea's silver doves."

Diana was the goddess of the hunt, but she was also the goddess of the Moon. In her guise as goddess of the Moon, she was known as Phoebe.

Venus, goddess of love, was born on the coast of the island of Cythera and so she was also known as Cytherea. Doves were sacred to her.

Aurelius continued, "I mean to make her my lovely bride, and in her bed to breathe the sweet content that I, as you know, for a long time have aimed at.

"Now, Valeria, it rests in you to help me to accomplish this so that I might gain my love. Your part you may perform easily if the merchant whom you told me of will, as he said he would, go to Alfonso's house, and say that he is my father, and also will pretend to pass over certain deeds of land to me so that I thereby may gain my heart's desire. I will pay the merchant for doing this."

"Fear not, my Lord," Valeria said. "I'll fetch him right away to you, for he'll do anything that you command. But tell me, my Lord, is Ferando married?"

"He is," Aurelius said, "and Polidor shortly shall be wed, and he intends to tame his wife before long."

"He *says* so," Valeria said, doubtfully.

"Indeed, he's gone to the taming school," Aurelius said.

"The taming school?" Valeria said. "Why, is there such a place?"

"Aye, and Ferando is the master of the school," Aurelius said.

"That's splendid," Valeria said, "but what method of taming does he use?"

"Indeed, I don't know, but he uses some odd device or other," Aurelius said. "But come, Valeria, I long to see the man, the merchant, whom we must use to accomplish our plotted goals, so that I may tell him what we have to do."

"Then come, my Lord," Valeria said, "and I will bring you to him immediately."

"Agreed," Aurelius said. "So then, let's go."

They exited.

— 3.3 —

Sander and his mistress, Kate, talked together in a room in Ferando's country house.

In this society, a mistress was a female house of household.

"Come, mistress," Sander said.

"Sander, please, help me to some food," Kate said. "I am so faint that I can scarcely stand."

"Aye, by the Virgin Mary, mistress," Sander said, "but you know my master has given me a standing order that you must eat nothing but that which he himself gives you."

"Why, man, your master need never know it!" Kate said.

"You say true, indeed," Sander said. "Why, look, mistress, what do you say to a piece of beef and mustard now?"

"Why, I say it is excellent food," Kate said. "Can you help me to some?"

"Aye, I could help you to some, but I fear that the mustard is too choleric for you," Sander said.

Mustard was thought to make people chloric: irritable and angry. Kate, of course, already possessed both of these characteristics.

Sander then asked, "But what do you say to a sheep's head and garlic?"

"Why, anything," Kate said. "I don't care what kind of food it is."

"Aye, but the garlic, I fear, will make your breath stink, and then my master will beat me for letting you eat it," Sander said. "But what do you say to a fat capon?"

A capon is a fattened castrated rooster.

"That's food for a king," Kate said. "Sweet Sander, help me to some of it."

44

"No, by our lady the Virgin Mary, if it's food for a king, then it is too expensive for us," Sander said. "We must not meddle with the king's food."

"Damn you, villain, do you mock me?" Kate yelled. "Take that for your sauciness."

She beat him.

"By God's wounds, are you so light-fingered that you are always ready to beat someone?" Sander said. "May a plague fall upon you! I'll keep you fasting for it these next two days!"

"I tell you, villain, I'll tear the flesh off your face and eat it, if you prattle to me like this!" Kate said.

"Here comes my master," Sander said. "Now he'll beat you."

Ferando entered the room with a piece of food upon his dagger's point. Polidor came with him.

"See here, Kate, I have provided food for you," Ferando said. "Here, take it. What, isn't it worthy of thanks?"

Kate refused to take the food.

Ferando said to Sander, "Go, Sirrah, take it away again."

Sander took the food, no doubt intending to eat it as soon as he was separated from Ferando.

Ferando said to Kate, "You shall be thankful for the next food you have."

Changing her mind about refusing the food, Kate said, "Why, I thank you for it."

"Nay, now it is not worth a pin," Ferando said.

He ordered Sander, "Go, Sirrah, and take it away, I say."

"Yes, sir, I'll carry it away," Sander said. "Master, let her have none, for she can fight, as hungry as she is."

"Please, sir, let it stand, for I'll eat some with her myself," Polidor said.

"Well, Sirrah, set it down again," Ferando said to Sander.

"Nay, nay, I ask you to let him take it away," Kate said. "I'll never be beholden to you for your food. I tell you flatly here to your teeth that you shall not keep me nor feed me as you wish, for I will go home again to my father's house."

"Aye, when you're meek and gentle, but not before," Ferando said. "I know your stomach — your pride — has not yet come down. Therefore, it is no marvel that you cannot eat. And I will go to your father's house.

"Come, Polidor, let us go in again.

"And, Kate, come in with us! I know before long that you and I shall lovingly agree."

They exited.

— 3.4 —

Aurelius, Valeria, and Phylotus the merchant talked together in the street in front of Alfonso's house. Phylotus the merchant had agreed to pretend to be Aurelius' father. Valeria was well dressed because he was wearing some of Aurelius' clothing.

"Now, Signior Phylotus," Aurelius said, "we will go to Alfonso's house. Be sure you say the things I told you concerning the man who dwells in Sestos, whose son I said I was, for you do very much resemble him. And fear not, you may be bold to speak your mind and adlib."

"I assure you, sir, that you need not worry," Phylotus the merchant said. "I'll act so cunningly and cleverly in the cause that you shall soon enjoy your heart's delight."

"Thanks, sweet Phylotus," Aurelius said. "Stay here, and I will go and fetch him here right away."

He and Valeria walked away a short distance, and Aurelius called, "Ho, Signior Alfonso, I request a word with you."

Alfonso came out of his house.

"Who's there?" Alfonso said. "What, Aurelius, what's the matter? Why do you stand so like a stranger at the door?"

"My father, sir, has newly come to town," Aurelius said, "and I have brought him here to speak with you concerning those matters that I told you of, and he can confirm the truth of everything I have said to you."

Looking at Phylotus the merchant, Alfonso asked, "Is this your father?"

Phylotus the merchant walked over to them.

Alfonso said, "You are welcome, sir."

"Thanks, Alfonso, for that's your name, I guess," Phylotus the merchant said. "I understand that my son has set his mind on and directed his liking to your daughter's love. And because he is my only son, and I gladly wish that he should do well, I tell you, sir, I do not mislike his choice.

"If you agree to give him your consent, he shall have wealth to maintain his high standard of living. Three hundred pounds a year I will give to him and to his heirs, and if he and your daughter join and knit themselves in holy wedlock, I will freely give him a thousand large ingots of pure gold, and twice as many bars of silver plate, and immediately I will confirm in writing what I have said in words."

"Trust me, I must commend your liberal and generous mind," Alfonso said, "and here I give him freely my consent. As for my daughter, I think he knows her mind: She returns his love. And I will enlarge her dowry for your sake; and celebrate with joy your nuptial rites."

Looking at Valeria, Alfonso then asked, "But is this gentleman from Sestos, too?"

Alfonso had seen Valeria before when he was Kate's music tutor, but Valeria was in disguise then, and so Alfonso did not now recognize the very well-dressed Valeria.

"He is the Duke of Sestos' thrice-renowned son, who for the love his honor bears to me has thus accompanied me to this place," Aurelius said.

Of course, Aurelius himself was the Duke of Sestos' son, but he was now pretending to be the son of a merchant of Sestos.

"You are to blame because you did not tell me earlier who he is," Alfonso said to Aurelius.

The son of a Duke is a very important person. If Alfonso had known that this man was the son of a Duke, he would have shown him respect earlier.

Aurelius then said to Valeria, who was pretending to be the son of a Duke, "Your honor would have been here in place with me. I would have done my duty to your honor."

"Thanks, good Alfonso," Valeria said, "but I came to see when these marriage rites would be performed. If in these nuptials you deign to honor thus the prince of Sestos' friend, he shall remain a lasting friend to you.

"What does Aurelius' father say?"

"I humbly thank your honor, my good Lord," Phylotus the merchant said, "and before we part, before your honor here, articles of such content shall be drawn between our houses and posterities — families and descendants — inviolate and pure on either part.

"With all my heart," Alfonso said, "and if your honor is pleased to walk along with us to my house, we will confirm these leagues of lasting love."

"Come then, Aurelius," Valeria said. "I will go with you."

They exited.

— 3.5 —

Ferando, Kate, and Sander talked together in a room in Ferando's country house.

"Master, the haberdasher has brought my mistress home her cap here," Sander said.

The haberdasher, who dealt in hats and caps, entered the room.

"Come here, Sirrah!" Ferando said. "What have you there?"

"A velvet cap, sir, if it please you," the haberdasher replied.

"Who ordered it?" Ferando asked. "Did you, Kate?"

"What if I did?" Kate replied.

She ordered the haberdasher, "Come here, Sirrah. Give me the cap! I'll see if it will fit me."

She tried on the velvet cap.

"Oh, monstrous," Ferando said. "Why, it does not become you. Let me see it, Kate!"

He snatched it from her head and gave it to the haberdasher, saying, "Here, Sirrah, take it away from here! This cap is quite out of fashion!"

"The fashion is good enough," Kate said. "Perhaps you mean to make a fool of me."

Of course, she meant that Ferando was trying to make a fool of her, but he deliberately misunderstood her.

He said, "Why, true, the haberdasher means to make a fool of you by having you put on such a tiny cap!

"Sirrah, begone with it!"

The haberdasher exited, holding the velvet cap.

A tailor holding a gown entered the room.

Sander said, "Here is the tailor, too, with my mistress' gown."

"Let me see it, tailor!" Ferando said. "What, with cuts and jags! By God's wounds, you villain, you have spoiled the gown!"

The gown had long cuts in it. Depending on the owner's preference, colored strips of cloth would be sewn into the cuts, or the cuts would be deliberately left in the gown so that the colored slip underneath the gown would be seen through the cuts.

"Why, sir, I made it as your serving-man Sander gave me instructions," the tailor said. "You may read the note here."

"Come here, Sirrah tailor!" Ferando said. "Read the note."

"Item, a fair round-compassed cape," the tailor read out loud.

The hem of the bottom of the cape formed a circle.

"Aye, that's correct," Sander said.

"And a large trunk sleeve," the tailor read out loud.

This kind of sleeve was baggy above the elbow and close-fitting below the elbow.

"That's a lie, master!" Sander said. "I said two trunk sleeves."

"Well, sir, continue!" Ferando said to the tailor.

"Item, a loose-bodied gown," the tailor said.

A loose-bodied gown is baggy, but Sander misunderstood or pretended to misunderstand "loose-bodied," taking it in the sense that the wearer of the gown — Kate — had a loose body (that is, she was a prostitute).

"Master, if ever I said loose body's gown, sew me in a seam and beat me to death with a ball of brown thread!" Sander said.

If Sander could be sewn into a seam, the gown was baggy, indeed.

"I made it as the note instructed me," the tailor said.

Sander said to the tailor, "I say the note lies in its throat, and you, too, if you say it."

"Nay, nay, never be so hot and angry, Sirrah," the tailor said, "for I don't fear you."

Tailors were supposed to be cowardly, but this tailor apparently was not cowardly.

"Do you hear, tailor?" Sander said. "You have braved many men. Don't brave me. You've faced many men."

"Braved" can mean "defied, stood up to," or it can mean "splendidly dressed."

"Faced" can mean "threatened," or it can mean "trimmed."

"Well, sir," the tailor said.

"Don't face me!" Sander said. "I'll be neither faced nor braved at your hands, I can tell you!"

"Come, come, I like the fashion of it well enough," Kate said. "Here's more trouble than is necessary. I'll have it, I will."

She then said to Ferando, "And if you do not like it, hide your eyes. I think I shall have nothing if I had to get it from you."

Ferando said to the tailor, "Go, I say, and take it up for your master's use."

Sander again deliberately misunderstood some words. By "take it up for your master's use," Ferando meant for the tailor to take the gown to his master for the master to do whatever he wanted with it. Sander pretended that the words meant to lift up the skirt of the gown in order to have sex with the woman wearing the gown.

"By God's wounds, villain, not for your life!" Sander said. "Don't touch it! By God's wounds, villain, take up my mistress' gown to his master's use!"

"Well, sir, what's your conceit of it?" Ferando asked Sander. "What do you mean?"

"I have a deeper conceit in it than you think," Sander said. "Take up my mistress' gown to his master's use!"

"Tailor, come here," Ferando said. "For this time take it away from here, and I'll content you for your pains. Take it away, but I will pay you for it."

"I thank you, sir," the tailor said.

The tailor exited, carrying the gown.

"Come, Kate, we now will go and see your father's house, even in these honest but mean articles of clothing," Ferando said.

Kate had apparently ordered the articles of clothing for her sisters' weddings.

Ferando continued, "Our purses shall be rich and our garments plain to protect our bodies from the winter rage, and that's enough. Why should we care for more?

"Your sisters, Kate, tomorrow must be wed, and I have promised them you would be there. The morning is well started; let's hasten away. It will be nine o'clock before we come there."

"Nine o'clock?" Kate said. "Why, it is already past two in the afternoon by all the clocks in the town!"

"I say it is only nine o'clock in the morning," Ferando said.

"I say it is two o'clock in the afternoon," Kate said.

"It shall be nine then before we go to your father's," Ferando said. "Come back again — we will not go today. Nothing but crossing of me still! I'll have you say as I do before you go."

They exited.

— 3.6 —

Polidor and Emelia, as well as Aurelius and Philema, talked together in a room in Alfonso's house.

Polidor said to his beloved, "Fair Emelia, summer's Sun-bright queen, brighter of hue than is the burning clime — the torrid zone — where Phoebus the Sun-god in the bright equator sits, creating gold and precious minerals.

"What would Emelia do, if I were forced to leave fair Athens and to wander the world?"

She replied, "Should you attempt to scale the seat of Jove, mounting the subtle airy regions, or be snatched up as formerly was Ganymede, love would give wings to my swift desires, and prompt my thoughts that I would follow you, or fall and perish as did Icarus."

Alfonso's daughters were educated. They knew much mythology.

The giants Otus and Ephialtes tried to scale Mount Olympus and make war against the gods. Their plan was to pile mountains on top of Mount Olympus; however, the Olympian gods defeated them and piled the mountains on top of Otus and Ephialtes.

Ganymede was a beautiful human boy whom Jupiter, aka Jove, King of the gods, kidnapped and made his cupbearer.

Icarus was the son of Daedalus, who designed the labyrinth at Crete to house the Minotaur, the half-bull, half-human man-eating monster. After Daedalus and his son were imprisoned on the island of Crete, Daedalus designed wings made of feathers and wax so that he and his son could fly over the sea to freedom. The wings worked, but Icarus flew too close to the Sun, the heat of which melted the wax, causing the feathers to molt. Icarus fell into the sea and drowned.

Aurelius said, "Sweetly answered, fair Emelia!"

He then said to his beloved, "But would Philema say as much to me, if I should ask a question now of you? What if the Duke of Sestos' only son" — whom Valeria was pretending to be; the disguised Aurelius himself was the Duke of Sestos' only son — "who came with me to your father's house, would seek to get Philema's love from me and make you duchess of that stately town. Wouldn't you then forsake me for his love?"

"Not for great Neptune, no, nor Jove himself, will Philema leave Aurelius' love," Philema answered. Even if he could make me empress of the world, or make me queen and guide of the heavens, yet I would not exchange your love for his.

"Your company is poor Philema's Heaven, and without you Heaven would be Hell to me."

Emelia and Philema now began a kind of contest with each proclaiming what they would do for their individual loves.

Emelia said, "And should my love, as once did Hercules, attempt to pass the burning vaults of Hell, I would with piteous looks and pleasing words, as once Orpheus did with his harmony and the ravishing sound of his melodious harp, entreat grim Pluto, god of the Land of the Dead, and from him obtain permission for you to go and safely return to the Land of the Living again."

Many ancient heroes entered Hell and safely returned again.

In one of his famous labors, Hercules entered Hell and carried away Cerberus, the three-headed guard dog. Hercules also entered Hell and rescued Theseus.

Orpheus mourned the death of Eurydice, his wife, so much that he went to the Land of the Dead in an attempt to bring her back to the Land of the Living. To get past Cerberus, the three-headed guard dog of Hell, he played his lute and sang. Cerberus, put under a spell by the music, fell asleep. Orpheus appeared before Pluto, the ruler of the Land of the Dead, and Proserpina, Pluto's queen, and he played sad music for them. Pluto agreed to let Eurydice return to the Land of the Living on one condition: Orpheus had to walk in front of her and not look at her until both he and his wife were in the Land of the Living. Orpheus led her up out of the Land of the Dead, but he was so eager to see her again that as soon as he stepped into the Land of the Living he turned around and looked at her. Unfortunately, Eurydice was still one step away from the Land of the Living. She said to him, "Farewell" — and disappeared.

Philema said, "And should my love, as formerly Leander did, attempt to swim the raging Hellespont for Hero's love, no towers of brass would hold me back, but I would follow you through those raging floods with my locks of hair all disheveled and my breast all bare. With bended knees on the shore of Abydos, where Leander lived, I would with smoky sighs and brinish tears importune Neptune and the watery gods to send a guard of silver-scaled dolphins with sounding Tritons to be our convoy, and to transport us safely to the shore, while I would hang about your lovely neck, redoubling kiss on kiss upon your cheeks, and with our pastime still the swelling waves."

Leander was the lover of the woman named Hero, a priestess of Venus. Leander swam across the Hellespont each night to visit her. She lit a lamp each night to guide his way across the narrow sea. One night, the winds blew out Hero's lamp, and Leander drowned. When Hero saw her lover's dead body, she committed suicide.

Danaë was a woman whom a tower could not keep away from a god who desired her. Danaë's father, Acrisius, heard a prophecy that her son would kill him, so he kept her shut away from men in a tower so that she would not become pregnant. Zeus, however, came to her in the form of golden rain and made her pregnant. Her father put her and her son, whose name was Perseus, in a chest and threw it into the sea. It washed ashore on an island. Much later, Perseus participated in athletic games and accidentally killed an old man with a wild throw of a javelin. That old man was Acrisius.

Tritons are minor sea-gods. They sound — blow — horns to calm rough seas.

Arion was captured by pirates. He played his cithera, a stringed musical instrument, and dolphins gathered around the pirate ship to hear the music. Arion then jumped into the sea, and a dolphin carried him on its back safely to shore.

Emelia said, "Should Polidor, as great Achilles did, only employ himself to follow arms and be a warrior, similar to the warlike Amazonian queen Penthesilea, Hector's paramour, who foiled the bloody Pyrrhus, murderous Greek, I'll thrust myself among the thickest throngs, and with my utmost force assist my love. I will go to battle with you and fight at your side."

Emelia got some things wrong in her allusions to mythology. Yes, Achilles was the greatest warrior in the Trojan War, but it was he, not Hector, who fell in love with Penthesilea. Also, Penthesilea did not foil Pyrrhus, Achilles' son. Penthesilea died in the Trojan War, but Pyrrhus survived.

Philema said, "Let Aeolus, god of the winds, storm, but let Aurelius be mild and quiet.

"Let Neptune, god of the sea, swell, but let Aurelius be calm and pleased.

"I don't care, whatever may happen: Let Fates and Fortune do the worst they can. I don't pay attention to them; they don't disagree with me, as long as my love and I do well agree."

Aurelius said, "Sweet Philema, you are beauty's mine and source of all beauty, from where the Sun exhales its glorious shine, and clads the heaven in your reflected rays!

"And now, my dearest love, the time draws near that Hymen, god of marriage, mounted in his saffron robe, must with his torches wait upon your wedding train, as Helen's brothers wait upon the horned crescent Moon."

In other words, it was time for Philema to get ready for the wedding that was soon to occur.

Helen's brothers are Castor and Pollux, who were turned into the constellation Gemini. At times, the constellation Gemini rises in the mid-northern latitudes with the Moon.

Aurelius continued, "Now, Juno, goddess of marriage, to your number I shall add the fairest bride whom any merchant ever had."

Polidor said, "Come, fair Emelia, the priest has gone, and at the church your father and the rest wait to see our marriage rites performed and see knit in sight of Heaven this Gordian knot that the teeth of fretting time may never untwist."

In a wedding ceremony, two people are knit — tied — together. The bond between Polidor and Emelia would be as tightly tied as the Gordian knot — a knot so intricate that people thought that it was impossible to untie. (Alexander the Great 'untied' the Gordian knot by cutting it in two with his sword.)

Polidor continued, "Then come, fair love, and celebrate with me this day's content and sweet ceremony."

They exited.

Sly asked, "Sim, must they be married now?"

The Lord replied, "Aye, my Lord."

CHAPTER 4

— 4.1 —

Ferando, Kate, and Sander entered the scene.

"Look, Sim, the fool has come again now," Sly said.

He was referring to Sander.

"Sirrah, go fetch our horses and bring them to the back gate right away," Ferando ordered.

"I will, sir, I promise you," Sander said.

He exited.

"Come, Kate," Ferando said. "The Moon shines clearly tonight, I think."

"The Moon?" Kate said. "Why, husband, you are deceived — it is the Sun!"

"Yet again?" Ferando said. "Come back again. It shall be the Moon before we go to your father's."

"Why, I'll say as you say," Kate said. "It is the Moon."

"Jesus save the glorious Moon!" Ferando said.

"Jesus save the glorious Moon!" Kate said.

"I am glad, Kate, that your stomach — your pride — has come down," Ferando said. "I know well that you know it is the Sun, but I tested you to see if you would speak and contradict me now, as you have done before. And trust me, Kate, had you not called it the Moon, we would have gone back again as surely as death.

"But wait, who is coming here?"

The Duke of Sestos, who was alone, entered the scene.

He said to himself, "Thus all alone from Sestos have I come. I left my princely court and noble train to come to Athens, and in this disguise, to see what course of life my son Aurelius takes.

"But wait, here's someone, it may be, who travels there."

He said, "Good sir, can you direct me the way to Athens?"

Ferando said to the Duke of Sestos, who was NOT disguised as a female, "Fair lovely maiden, young and affable, you are more clear of hue and far more beautiful than precious sardonyx or purple amethysts, or glistening hyacinth! You are more amiable by far than is the plain where glistening Cepheus in silver bowers gazes upon the giant Andromeda!"

Cepheus and Andromeda are constellations. Andromeda is a much larger constellation than Cepheus.

Like many constellations, Andromeda and Cepheus have a basis in mythology. Cepheus was a King of Ethiopia in Greek mythology, and Andromeda was his daughter. Cepheus offended the Nereids — sea-goddesses — by claiming that Andromeda was more beautiful than they were. They complained to Neptune, god of the sea, and he sent a sea-monster to devastate Cepheus' kingdom. Perseus, traveling while mounted on his winged horse Pegasus, saw and fell in love with Andromeda and killed the sea-monster.

Ferando then said, "Sweet Kate, entertain this lovely woman."

"I think the man is mad," the Duke of Sestos said. "He calls me a woman."

Kate said, "Fair lovely lady, bright and crystalline, beauteous and stately as the eye-trained bird — the peacock, which has eyes in its train of feathers — as glorious as the dew-washed morning, within whose eyes the morning takes her dawning beams, and golden summer sleeps upon your cheeks, wrap up your radiating light and heat in some cloud, lest your beauty make this stately town uninhabitable like the burning zone of the equator with the sweet reflections of your lovely face!"

"What! Is she mad, too?" the Duke of Sestos said to himself. "Or is my shape so transformed that both of them convince me that I am a woman? But they are mad, surely, and therefore I'll be gone, and leave their company for fear of harm, and hasten to Athens to seek my son."

The Duke of Sestos exited.

Ferando said, "Why, so, Kate; this was done in a friendly way by you, and kindly, too. Why, thus must we two live: one mind, one heart, and one happiness for both for us!

"And glad he is, I am sure, that he has gone. But come, sweet Kate, for we will go after him and this time we will convince him that he is a man again."

They exited.

— 4.2 —

Alfonso, Phylotus the merchant, Valeria, Polidor, Emelia, Aurelius, and Philema spoke together on a street in Athens. Polidor and Emilia were just married, as were Aurelius and Philema.

"Come, lovely sons," Alfonso said. "Your marriage rites have been performed, so let's hurry home to see what celebratory food and drink we have. I wonder that Ferando and his wife have not come to see this great celebration."

"It's no marvel if Ferando is away," Polidor said. "His wife, Kate, I think, has so troubled his wits that he remains at home to keep them warm. Forward wedlock, as the proverb says, had brought him to his nightcap long ago."

The word "forward" means "eager" or "well-advanced."

A proverb of the time stated, "Age and wedlock bring a man to his nightcap." In other words: Old men and married men prefer to stay at home and go to bed rather than to go out and carouse all night.

Phylotus the merchant, who was pretending to be Aurelius' father, said, "But, Polidor, let my son and you take heed that Ferando not say before long as much to you.

"And now, Alfonso, the more to show my love to you, if to Sestos you send your ships, I myself will load them with Arabian silks, rich African spices, arras, counter-points, musk, cassia, sweet-smelling ambergris, pearl, coral, crystal, jet lignite, and ivory to celebrate the favors you have given to my son and the friendly love that you have shown to him."

Arras are wall hangings, and counter-points are quilts.

Cassia is an aromatic shrub, and ambergris is an aromatic secretion of the sperm whale that is used in the fragrance industry. Cassia cinnamon is widely consumed, and ambergris can be worth thousands of dollars an ounce.

The Duke of Sestos entered the scene and listened without being noticed.

Valeria, who was pretending to be the Duke of Sestos' son, and whom the Duke recognized because Valeria was one of his serving-men, said, "And in order to honor him and this fair bride, I'll yearly send you from my father's court several chests of refined sugar, ten barrels of Tunisian wine, sweetmeats, and sweet-smelling substances to celebrate and observe this day. And your merchants shall trade custom-free and by so doing increase the profits of your land, sending you gold for brass, silver for lead, and cases of silk for packs of wool and cloth to bind this friendship and confirm this league."

The Duke of Sestos spoke up: "I am glad, sir, that you would be so frank. Have you become the Duke of Sestos' son, and do you revel with my treasure in this town? Base villain, that thus you dishonor me!"

Valeria thought, *By God's wounds, it is the Duke! What shall I do?*

He decided to brave it out: "Dishonor you? Why, do you know what you are saying?"

"Here's no villain!" the Duke of Sestos said sarcastically. "He will not know me now!"

He then said to Aurelius, "But what do you say? Have you forgotten me, too?"

Phylotus, who was pretending to be Aurelius' merchant father (not the Duke), said, "Why, sir, are you acquainted with my son?"

"With your son?" the Duke of Sestos said. "No, trust me, if he is yours."

He then spoke again to Aurelius, his son: "Please tell me, sir, who am I?"

Aurelius knelt in supplication to his father and said, "Pardon me, father! Humbly on my knees, I entreat your grace to hear me speak."

"Peace, villain!" the angry Duke of Sestos said.

Referring to Valeria and Phylotus the merchant, the Duke of Sestos said, "Lay hands on them, and send them to prison immediately."

Valeria and Phylotus the merchant ran away.

Sly said, "I say that we'll have no sending to prison."

The Lord replied, "My Lord, this is just a play; they're only doing this in jest."

"I tell you, Sim, we'll have no sending to prison, that's for sure," Sly said. "Why, Sim, am not I Don Christo Vary?"

He had made up a fancy name for himself. "Don" is a Spanish title. "Christo" refers to Christ. "Vary" can refer to "variation." He was certainly a variation when compared to a real Spanish Christian Lord.

Sly continued, "Therefore, I say, they shall not go to prison."

"They shall not go to prison, my Lord," the real Lord said. "They have run away."

"Have they run away, Sim?" Sly said. "That's well. Then give us some more drink, and let the actors play again."

"Here, my Lord!" the real Lord said, filling his cup.

Sly drank and then fell asleep.

The Duke of Sestos said to his son, "Ah, treacherous boy, who dared presume to get married without your father's permission!

"I swear by fair Cynthia's burning rays, by Merops' head, and by the seven-mouthed Nile River, that if I had but known about this, before you had wedded her, then this angry sword of mine would have ripped your hateful chest even if the world's immortal soul resided in your breast and it would have hewed you into pieces smaller than the sands of the Libyan desert."

Cynthia is a name for the Moon-goddess.

Merops was the husband of Clymene, who gave birth to Phaëthon, whose father was the Sun-god. Phaëthon went to his father, the god

Apollo, and asked to be allowed to drive the Sun-chariot across the sky and bring light to the world. But Phaëthon, doomed youth, was unable to control the stallions, and they ran wildly away with the Sun-chariot, wreaking havoc and destruction upon Humankind and the world. The King of the gods, Jupiter, saved Humankind and the world by throwing a thunderbolt at Phaëthon and killing him.

The Duke of Sestos continued criticizing his son, who was hanging his head in shame, "Turn your face toward me, oh, cruel, impious boy!"

He then said, "Alfonso, I did not think you would presume to match your daughter with my princely house and never make me acquainted with the fact."

Alfonso said, "My Lord, by the heavens I swear to your grace, I knew none other but that Valeria, your serving-man, had been the Duke of Sestos' noble son. Nor did my daughter, I dare swear for her. We truly believed that Valeria was the son of the Duke of Sestos."

Referring to Valeria, who was supposed to keep Aurelius out of trouble, the Duke of Sestos said, "That damned villain who has deluded me, whom I sent to be a guide to my son! Oh, that my furious force could cleave the earth, so that I might muster battalions of Hellish fiends to rack his heart and tear his impious soul. The ceaseless turning of the celestial orbs does not kindle greater flames in flitting air than does the passionate anguish of my raging breast."

This society believed in Ptolemaic astronomy, in which the planets, stars, and Sun were embedded in crystalline celestial orbs or spheres that rotated around the Earth.

Aurelius now mentioned some near-impossible tasks, including the killing of the Hydra, that he would be willing to perform if his father would forgive him once they were accomplished.

Hercules' second labor was killing the Lernaean Hydra. In accomplishing this labor, Hercules had the help of a nephew named Iolaus. The Hydra of Lerna had nine heads, the middle of which was immortal. Hercules and Iolaus traveled to Lerna and found the Hydra's lair. Hercules forced the Hydra to leave its lair by shooting flaming arrows into the lair. Hercules fought the Hydra, but he discovered that each time a mortal head was cut off, two more heads grew in its place. Hera gave Hercules even more trouble by sending an enormous crab to fight him, but Hercules crushed the crab. Hercules then got help from Iolaus. Each time Hercules cut off one of the Hydra's mortal heads, Iolaus cauterized it with a torch, thus preventing more heads from growing. Hercules then cut off the immortal head and placed it under a boulder. The blood of the Hydra was poisonous, and before leaving, Hercules dipped the heads of his arrows into the Hydra's blood.

Aurelius, repentant, said, "Then let my death, sweet father, end your grief. For I it is who thus have wrought your woes. So then be revenged on me, for here I swear that these others are innocent of what I did. Oh, if I had the charge to cut off the Hydra's head, to make the topless Alps a level field, to kill untamed monsters with my sword, to travail daily in the hottest Sun, and to watch in winter when the nights are cold, I would with gladness undertake them all and think the pain is only pleasure that I felt, as long as my noble father at my return would forget and pardon my offence!"

Philema, Aurelius' wife, knelt before the Duke of Sestos and said, "Let me entreat your grace upon my knees to pardon your son and let my death discharge the heavy wrath your grace has vowed against him."

Polidor, Aurelius' friend, knelt before the Duke of Sestos and said, "My good Lord, let us entreat your grace to purge your stomach of this melancholy: Taint not your princely mind with grief, my Lord, but pardon and forgive these lovers' faults, who kneeling before you now crave your gracious favor here."

Emelia said, "Great prince of Sestos, let a woman's words entreat a pardon in your Lordly breast, both for your princely son, and us, my Lord."

The Duke of Sestos, forgiving his son, said, "Aurelius, stand up. I pardon you. I see that virtue will have enemies, and Lady Fortune will be thwarting honor always."

He then said to Philema, "And you, fair virgin, too, I am content to accept you for my daughter-in-law, since the wedding is done, and I will see that you are treated like a member of the royal family in Sestos' court."

"Thanks, my good Lord," Philema said, "and I no longer live than I obey and honor you in everything."

Alfonso said, "Let me give thanks to your royal grace for this great honor done to me and mine. If your grace will walk into my house, I will, in the humblest manner I can, show the eternal service I do owe your grace."

"Thanks, good Alfonso," the Duke of Sestos said, "but I came alone, and not as befits the Sestian Duke. Nor would I have it known within the town that I was here without my train of attendants. As I came alone, so will I go, and leave my son to celebrate his feast.

"Before long I'll come again to you and do him honor as befits the son of mighty Jerobel, Duke of Sestos, until the time when I'll leave you."

He then said, "Farewell, Aurelius!"

"Not yet, my Lord," Aurelius said. "I'll accompany you to your ship."

The actors exited.

The Lord noticed that Sly was asleep, and he called for some serving-men: "Who's within there?

"Come here, sirs, my Lord's asleep again. Go and pick him gently up, and put his own apparel on him again, and lay him in the place where we found him, near the alehouse. But see that you don't wake him for any reason."

"It shall be done, my Lord," the boy-servant said.

The boy-servant then said to the serving-men, "Come, help to carry him away from here."

They all exited with the serving-men carrying Sly.

65

CHAPTER 5
— 5.1 —

Ferando and his serving-man Sander, Aurelius and his serving-man Valeria, and Polidor and his boy-servant were gathered together in a room in Alfonso's house.

Ferando said, "Come, gentlemen, now that supper's over, how shall we spend the time until we go to bed?"

"Indeed," Aurelius said, "if you will, we will spend it in a test of our wives to see who will come soonest at her husband's call."

"Nay," Polidor said, "if we do that, then Ferando must necessarily sit it out, or he may call, I think, until he is weary before his wife will come before she wishes to come to him."

"It is well for you who have such gentle wives," Ferando said, "yet I will not sit out this test. Kate may come as soon as your wives."

Aurelius said, "I bet a hundred pounds that my wife will come soonest."

"I'll take that bet," Polidor said. "I'll bet as much as you — a hundred pounds — that my wife comes as soon as I send for her."

"How do you feel now, Ferando?" Aurelius said. "Perhaps you dare not bet?"

Ferando replied, "Why, true, I dare not bet indeed — but why dare I not bet? I dare not bet so little money on so sure a thing. A hundred pounds! Why, I have bet as much upon my dog, in running at a deer. My wife, Kate, shall not come so far for such a trifle of money.

"But will you bet five hundred marks with me on whose wife will soonest come when he calls for her and shows herself to be most loving to him? Let him who wins enjoy the money from the wager I have laid!

"Now, what do you say? Do you dare to risk five hundred marks?"

Aurelius shook his head no and stayed quiet, but Polidor replied, "Aye, and I would even if the wager were for a thousand pounds. I dare to presume on my wife's love, and I will bet with you. My wife loves me so much that she will come quickly if I call for her."

Alfonso entered the scene and said, "How are you now, sons? What! Having such an intense conversation? May I, without offence, know what your conversation is about?"

"Indeed, father," Aurelius said, "we are having a weighty argument about our wives. Five hundred marks already we have bet, and he whose wife shows the most love to him will enjoy all the winnings."

"Why, then, Ferando is sure to lose!" Alfonso said.

He then said to Ferando, "I promise you, son, that your wife will hardly come when you call for her, and therefore I wish you would not bet so much money."

"Tush, father," Ferando said, "even if it were ten times more, I would dare risk it on my lovely Kate and her obedience."

He then said to Aurelius and Polidor, "But if I lose, I'll pay; and so shall you."

"Upon my honor," Aurelius said, "if I lose, I'll pay."

"And so will I," Polidor said. "Upon my faith, I vow that I'll pay."

"Then let's sit down and send for our wives," Ferando said.

"I tell you truly, Ferando," Alfonso said. "I am afraid you will lose."

Aurelius said, "I'll send for my wife first.

"Valeria, go bid your mistress — my wife — to come to me."

Exiting, Valeria said, "I will, my Lord."

"Now for my hundred pounds!" Aurelius said. "If anyone would bet ten hundred more pounds with me, I know I should obtain it by her love."

This was bravado. Ferando had offered to bet five hundred marks, but Aurelius had not accepted that bet.

Ferando said, "I pray to God that you have not bet too much already."

"Trust me, Ferando," Aurelius said. "I am sure that you have bet too much already, for you, I dare to presume, have lost it all."

Valeria re-entered the scene.

Aurelius asked, "Now, Sirrah, what does your mistress say?"

Valeria replied, "She says that she is somewhat busy, but she'll come soon."

"Why, so it goes," Ferando said. "Didn't I tell you this before? She is busy and cannot come."

"I pray to God your wife will send you so good an answer!" Aurelius said.

He believed that Kate was going to send Ferando a much ruder refusal to come.

Aurelius continued, "She may be busy, yet she says she'll come."

"Well, well!" Ferando said. "Polidor, send for your wife."

"Agreed!" Polidor said. "Boy, desire your mistress to come here."

Exiting, his boy-servant said, "I will, sir."

"Aye, so, so," Ferando said. "He 'desires' her to come."

Aurelius and Polidor had used words — "bid" and "desire" — that were politer than "command."

"Polidor, I dare presume for you that I think your wife will not refuse to come," Alfonso said. "And I marvel much, Aurelius, that your wife did not come when you sent for her."

The boy-servant returned.

Polidor asked, "Now where's your mistress — my wife?"

"She told me to tell you that she will not come," the boy-servant said. "If you have any business with her, you must come to her."

"Oh, monstrous, intolerable presumption," Ferando said. "This is worse than a blazing star — an evil-omened comet. This is worse than snow at midsummer, earthquakes, or anything that is unseasonable and unsuitable! She will not come; instead, he must come to her."

"Well, sir, I request of you, let's hear what answer your wife will make to your request for her to come to you," Polidor said.

Ferando said to Sander, "Sirrah, command your mistress to come to me immediately."

Sander exited.

"I think my wife, although she did not come, will prove to be the kindest of the three wives, for now I have no fear," Aurelius said. "I am sure Ferando's wife will not come."

Aurelius' wife had at least said that she would come soon. Aurelius expected that that would the best response made by the three wives.

"The more's the pity," Ferando said. "Then I must lose."

Kate and Sander entered the scene.

Ferando continued, "But I have won, for see where Kate is coming!"

"Sweet husband," Kate said, "did you send for me?"

"I did, my love," Ferando said. "I sent for you to come. Come here, Kate, what's that upon your head?"

"Nothing, husband, but my cap, I think," Kate said.

"Pull it off, and tread it under your feet," Ferando said. "It is foolish, and I will not have you wear it."

Kate took off her cap, threw it on the ground, and trod on it.

"Oh, wonderful metamorphosis!" an astonished Polidor said.

"This is a wonder almost past belief!" an astonished Aurelius said.

"This is a token of her true love to me," Ferando said, "and yet I'll test her further; you shall see."

He then said to Kate, "Come hither, Kate. Where are your sisters-in-law?"

"They are sitting in the bridal chamber," Kate said.

"Fetch them here," Ferando said, "and if they will not come, bring them here by force and make them come with you."

"I will," Kate said.

She exited.

"I promise you, Ferando," Alfonso said. "I would have sworn that your wife would never have done so much for and been so obedient to you."

"But you shall see that she will do more than this," Ferando said, "for see where she brings her sisters forth by force!"

Kate entered the room, thrusting Philema and Emelia before her, making them come to their husbands' call.

"See, husband, I have brought them both," Kate said.

"It is well done, Kate," Ferando said.

"Aye, to be sure," Emelia said, "and done like a loving masterpiece; you're worthy to have great praise for this feat."

"Aye, for making a fool of herself and us," Philema said.

"Curse you, Philema, you have lost me a hundred pounds tonight," Aurelius said, "because I bet that you would be the first to have come to her husband's call."

"But you, Emelia, have lost me a great deal more," Polidor said.

Aurelius had bet only one hundred pounds, while Polidor had bet five hundred marks. A mark was worth two-thirds of a pound sterling.

"You might have kept it better then," Emelia said. "Who told you to make that bet?"

"Now, lovely Kate," Ferando said, "before their husbands here, I want you to please tell these headstrong women what duty wives owe to their husbands."

Kate said, "You who live by your pampered wills, even disobeying your husbands, now listen to me and carefully note what I shall say.

"The eternal Power with only His breath shall cause this end and has framed this beginning, not in time, nor before time, but with time, bringing chaos."

The first stage of creation was chaos, which was followed by God's bringing order out of chaos.

Kate continued, "For all the courses of years, of ages, of months, of temperate seasons, of days and hours are tuned and stopped by the measure of His hand."

God is like a skilled musician as He controls time. The word "stopped" refers to pressing on the strings of a musical instrument.

Kate continued, "The first world was a form without a form, a confused heap, a mixture all deformed, a gulf of gulfs, a bodiless body, where all the elements were without order. This was before the great Commander of the World, the King of Kings, the glorious God of Heaven in six days framed His heavenly work and made all things stand in perfect course.

"Then in His image He made a man, Old Adam, and from his side when he was asleep, the Lord took a rib from which He did make the woe of man, so termed by Adam then wo-man, because sin came to us through her, and because of her sin Adam was doomed to die."

Eve, the first woman, committed the first sin: the eating of the Forbidden Fruit in the Garden of Eden. Eve first ate the Forbidden Fruit, and then she tempted Adam to also eat the Forbidden Fruit.

Kate then referred to Sarah, the wife of Abraham. 1 Peter 3:6 recommends that wives should behave toward their spouses "As Sara obeyed Abraham, and called him Sir" (Geneva Bible of 1561).

Kate continued, "As Sarah to her husband, so should we obey them, love them, keep them, and nourish them if they by any means want our helps. We should lay our hands under their feet to tread on if by doing that we might procure their ease, and for a precedent I'll first begin and lay my hand under my husband's feet."

She lay her hand under her husband's feet.

Why only one hand and not both? Laying both hands under her husband's feet apparently would not have procured his ease. Ferando had said more than once that Kate would rule once she had been tamed. Presumably they would share the rule, perhaps not equally, but with Kate having much influence when they made decisions.

Ferando's taming may have benefited Kate. Living life as a shrew may not be a good life. Living with a husband whom one respects can be a good life.

"Enough, sweetheart, you have won the wager," Ferando said. "And they, I am sure, cannot deny that you have won the wager."

"Aye, Ferando, you have won the wager," Alfonso said. "And to show you how I am pleased in this, I freely give you a hundred pounds more — another dowry for another daughter, for she is not the same daughter she was before."

Kate had changed remarkably, and she did not resemble the shrew that she had been before.

"Thanks, sweet father," Ferando said. "Gentlemen, good night, for Kate and I will leave you for tonight. Kate and I are wed, and you are sped, and so, farewell, for we will go to our beds."

The word "sped" meant "defeated."

Ferando, Kate, and Sander exited.

"Now, Aurelius, what do you say to this?" Alfonso asked.

"Believe me, father, I rejoice to see that Ferando and his wife so lovingly agree," Aurelius said.

Aurelius, Philema, Alfonso, and Valeria exited.

"How are you now, Polidor? In a dump? Depressed? What do you say, man?" Emelia asked.

"I say you are a shrew," Polidor said.

"That's better than a sheep," Emelia replied.

"Well, since it is done, let it go," Polidor said. "Come, let's go in."

They exited.

EPILOGUE

Two of the Lord's serving-men carried Sly, who was dressed in his own clothes again, to the alehouse, and they left him where they found him, and exited.

The bartender came out of the alehouse and said, "Now that the dark night has passed, and dawning day appears in crystal sky, now must I hasten abroad.

"But wait, who's this?

"What! Sly? Oh, wondrous, has he lain here all night? I'll wake him up. I think he would have starved by this time except that his belly was so stuffed with ale.

"What! How! Sly! Wake up! For shame!"

Awakened, Sly said, "Give us some more wine! What! Are all the actors gone? Am not I a Lord?"

"A Lord! You must be joking!" the bartender said. "Come, are you still drunken?"

"Who's this?" Sly said. "The bartender? Oh, Lord, Sirrah, I have had the most splendid dream tonight that you ever heard in all your life!"

"Aye, by the Virgin Mary," the bartender said, "but you had best get yourself home, for your wife will beat you for dreaming here tonight."

"Will she?" Sly said. "I know now how to tame a shrew! I dreamt about it all this night until now, and you have waked me out of the best dream that I ever had in my life. But I will go to my wife right away, and I will tame her, too, if she angers me."

"Nay, wait, Sly," the bartender said, "for I'll go home with you, and hear the rest that you have dreamt tonight."

APPENDIX A: NOTES

— 3.6 —

That Hymen mounted in his saffron robe,
*   Must with his torches wait upon thy train,*
*   As Helen's brothers on the hornèd moon. – (74-76)*
The below passage comes from earthsky.org:

On November 5 and 6, 2020, before going to bed look for the moon in your eastern sky. It'll be a bright waning gibbous moon, and you might notice two bright stars in its vicinity. These stars are noticeable for being both bright and close together on the sky's dome, and that is why — in legends of the sky — they often represent Twins.

The stars are Castor and Pollux in the constellation Gemini.

From mid-northern latitudes, they appear over your eastern horizon with the moon by around 9 p.m. on November 6. The next day – on November 6 – Castor and Pollux will rise about 4 minutes earlier whereas the moon will come up about one hour later. From the Southern Hemisphere, they all ascend in the east a bit later in the evening. If you're not one for staying up late, you can always get up before dawn to view the moon and Gemini stars in the morning sky. Then they'll be in the west!

Source: Bruce McClure, "Watch for the moon and the Twins." earthsky.org. 5 November 2020 <https://earthsky.org/?p=86583>.

Note: A waning gibbous moon is not a horned — crescent — moon.

—4.1 —

More amiable far than is the plain
*   Where glistering Cepherus in silver bowers,*

Gazeth upon the giant Andromede! (4.1.45-47)

The below passage comes from the Wikipedia article on "Andromeda (constellation)":

> *Andromeda is one of the 48 constellations listed by the 2nd-century Greco-Roman astronomer Ptolemy and remains one of the 88 modern constellations. [...]*
>
> *Its brightest star, Alpha Andromedae, is a binary star that has also been counted as a part of Pegasus, while Gamma Andromedae is a colorful binary and a popular target for amateur astronomers. Only marginally dimmer than Alpha, Beta Andromedae is a red giant, its color visible to the naked eye. The constellation's most obvious deep-sky object is the naked-eye Andromeda Galaxy (M31, also called the Great Galaxy of Andromeda), the closest spiral galaxy to the Milky Way and one of the brightest Messier objects. Several fainter galaxies, including M31's companions M110 and M32, as well as the more distant NGC 891, lie within Andromeda. The Blue Snowball Nebula, a planetary nebula, is visible in a telescope as a blue circular object.*

Part of the constellation Andromeda is a giant galaxy called either the Andromeda Galaxy or the Great Galaxy of Andromeda. This galaxy can be seen with the naked eye.

Of course, when *The Taming of a Shrew* was written, people had no idea of galaxies. Nevertheless, this is interesting.

APPENDIX B: ABOUT THE AUTHOR

It was a dark and stormy night. Suddenly a cry rang out, and on a hot summer night in 1954, Josephine, wife of Carl Bruce, gave birth to a boy — me. Unfortunately, this young married couple allowed Reuben Saturday, Josephine's brother, to name their first-born. Reuben, aka "The Joker," decided that Bruce was a nice name, so he decided to name me Bruce Bruce. I have gone by my middle name — David — ever since.

Being named Bruce David Bruce hasn't been all bad. Bank tellers remember me very quickly, so I don't often have to show an ID. It can be fun in charades, also. When I was a counselor as a teenager at Camp Echoing Hills in Warsaw, Ohio, a fellow counselor gave the signs for "sounds like" and "two words," then she pointed to a bruise on her leg twice. Bruise Bruise? Oh yeah, Bruce Bruce is the answer!

Uncle Reuben, by the way, gave me a haircut when I was in kindergarten. He cut my hair short and shaved a small bald spot on the back of my head. My mother wouldn't let me go to school until the bald spot grew out again.

Of all my brothers and sisters (six in all), I am the only transplant to Athens, Ohio. I was born in Newark, Ohio, and have lived all around Southeastern Ohio. However, I moved to Athens to go to Ohio University and have never left.

At Ohio U, I never could make up my mind whether to major in English or Philosophy, so I got a Bachelor's with a double major in both areas in 1980, then I added a Master's in English in 1984 and a Master's in Philosophy in 1985. Currently, I am a retired English instructor at Ohio U.

If all goes well, I will publish one or two books a year for the rest of my life. (On the other hand, a good way to make God laugh is to tell Her your plans.)

By the way, my sister Brenda Kennedy writes romances such as *A New Beginning* and *Shattered Dreams*.

APPENDIX C: SOME BOOKS BY DAVID BRUCE

Retellings of a Classic Work of Literature

Arden of Faversham: A Retelling

Ben Jonson's The Alchemist: *A Retelling*

Ben Jonson's The Arraignment, or Poetaster: *A Retelling*

Ben Jonson's Bartholomew Fair: *A Retelling*

Ben Jonson's The Case is Altered: *A Retelling*

Ben Jonson's Catiline's Conspiracy: *A Retelling*

Ben Jonson's The Devil is an Ass: *A Retelling*

Ben Jonson's Epicene: *A Retelling*

Ben Jonson's Every Man in His Humor: *A Retelling*

Ben Jonson's Every Man Out of His Humor: *A Retelling*

Ben Jonson's The Fountain of Self-Love, or Cynthia's Revels: *A Retelling*

Ben Jonson's The Magnetic Lady, or Humors Reconciled: *A Retelling*

Ben Jonson's The New Inn, or The Light Heart: *A Retelling*

Ben Jonson's Sejanus' Fall: *A Retelling*

Ben Jonson's The Staple of News: *A Retelling*

Ben Jonson's A Tale of a Tub: *A Retelling*

Ben Jonson's Volpone, or the Fox: *A Retelling*

Christopher Marlowe's Complete Plays: Retellings

Christopher Marlowe's Dido, Queen of Carthage: *A Retelling*

Christopher Marlowe's Doctor Faustus: *Retellings of the 1604 A-Text and of the 1616 B-Text*

Christopher Marlowe's Edward II: *A Retelling*

Christopher Marlowe's The Massacre at Paris: *A Retelling*

Christopher Marlowe's The Rich Jew of Malta: *A Retelling*

Christopher Marlowe's Tamburlaine, Parts 1 and 2: *Retellings*

Dante's Divine Comedy: *A Retelling in Prose*

Dante's Inferno: *A Retelling in Prose*

Dante's Purgatory: *A Retelling in Prose*

Dante's Paradise: *A Retelling in Prose*

The Famous Victories of Henry V: *A Retelling*

From the Iliad *to the* Odyssey: *A Retelling in Prose of Quintus of Smyrna's* Posthomerica

George Chapman, Ben Jonson, and John Marston's Eastward Ho! *A Retelling*

George Peele's The Arraignment of Paris: *A Retelling*

George Peele's The Battle of Alcazar: *A Retelling*

George Peele's David and Bathsheba, and the Tragedy of Absalom: *A Retelling*

George Peele's Edward I: *A Retelling*

George Peele's The Old Wives' Tale: *A Retelling*

George-a-Greene: *A Retelling*

The History of King Leir: *A Retelling*

Homer's Iliad: *A Retelling in Prose*

Homer's Odyssey: *A Retelling in Prose*

J.W. Gent.'s The Valiant Scot: *A Retelling*

Jason and the Argonauts: A Retelling in Prose of Apollonius of Rhodes' Argonautica

John Ford: Eight Plays Translated into Modern English

John Ford's The Broken Heart: *A Retelling*

John Ford's The Fancies, Chaste and Noble: *A Retelling*

John Ford's The Lady's Trial: *A Retelling*

John Ford's The Lover's Melancholy: *A Retelling*

John Ford's Love's Sacrifice: *A Retelling*

John Ford's Perkin Warbeck: *A Retelling*

John Ford's The Queen: *A Retelling*

John Ford's 'Tis Pity She's a Whore: *A Retelling*

John Lyly's Campaspe: *A Retelling*

John Lyly's Endymion, The Man in the Moon: *A Retelling*

John Lyly's Galatea: *A Retelling*

John Lyly's Love's Metamorphosis: *A Retelling*

John Lyly's Midas: *A Retelling*

John Lyly's Mother Bombie: *A Retelling*

John Lyly's Sappho and Phao: *A Retelling*

John Lyly's The Woman in the Moon: *A Retelling*

John Webster's The White Devil: *A Retelling*

King Edward III: *A Retelling*

Mankind: *A Medieval Morality Play* (A Retelling)

Margaret Cavendish's The Unnatural Tragedy: *A Retelling*

The Merry Devil of Edmonton: *A Retelling*

The Summoning of Everyman: *A Medieval Morality Play* (A Retelling)

Robert Greene's Friar Bacon and Friar Bungay: *A Retelling*

The Taming of a Shrew: *A Retelling*

Tarlton's Jests: A Retelling

Thomas Middleton's A Chaste Maid in Cheapside: *A Retelling*

Thomas Middleton's Women Beware Women: *A Retelling*

Thomas Middleton and Thomas Dekker's The Roaring Girl: *A Retelling*
Thomas Middleton and William Rowley's The Changeling: *A Retelling*
The Trojan War and Its Aftermath: Four Ancient Epic Poems
Virgil's Aeneid: *A Retelling in Prose*
William Shakespeare's 5 Late Romances: Retellings in Prose
William Shakespeare's 10 Histories: Retellings in Prose
William Shakespeare's 11 Tragedies: Retellings in Prose
William Shakespeare's 12 Comedies: Retellings in Prose
William Shakespeare's 38 Plays: Retellings in Prose
William Shakespeare's 1 Henry IV, aka Henry IV, Part 1: *A Retelling in Prose*
William Shakespeare's 2 Henry IV, aka Henry IV, Part 2: *A Retelling in Prose*
William Shakespeare's 1 Henry VI, aka Henry VI, Part 1: *A Retelling in Prose*
William Shakespeare's 2 Henry VI, aka Henry VI, Part 2: *A Retelling in Prose*
William Shakespeare's 3 Henry VI, aka Henry VI, Part 3: *A Retelling in Prose*
William Shakespeare's All's Well that Ends Well: *A Retelling in Prose*
William Shakespeare's Antony and Cleopatra: *A Retelling in Prose*
William Shakespeare's As You Like It: *A Retelling in Prose*
William Shakespeare's The Comedy of Errors: *A Retelling in Prose*
William Shakespeare's Coriolanus: *A Retelling in Prose*
William Shakespeare's Cymbeline: *A Retelling in Prose*
William Shakespeare's Hamlet: *A Retelling in Prose*
William Shakespeare's Henry V: *A Retelling in Prose*
William Shakespeare's Henry VIII: *A Retelling in Prose*
William Shakespeare's Julius Caesar: *A Retelling in Prose*
William Shakespeare's King John: *A Retelling in Prose*
William Shakespeare's King Lear: *A Retelling in Prose*
William Shakespeare's Love's Labor's Lost: *A Retelling in Prose*
William Shakespeare's Macbeth: *A Retelling in Prose*
William Shakespeare's Measure for Measure: *A Retelling in Prose*
William Shakespeare's The Merchant of Venice: *A Retelling in Prose*
William Shakespeare's The Merry Wives of Windsor: *A Retelling in Prose*
William Shakespeare's A Midsummer Night's Dream: *A Retelling in Prose*
William Shakespeare's Much Ado About Nothing: *A Retelling in Prose*
William Shakespeare's Othello: *A Retelling in Prose*
William Shakespeare's Pericles, Prince of Tyre: *A Retelling in Prose*
William Shakespeare's Richard II: *A Retelling in Prose*
William Shakespeare's Richard III: *A Retelling in Prose*
William Shakespeare's Romeo and Juliet: *A Retelling in Prose*
William Shakespeare's The Taming of the Shrew: *A Retelling in Prose*

William Shakespeare's The Tempest: *A Retelling in Prose*
William Shakespeare's Timon of Athens: *A Retelling in Prose*
William Shakespeare's Titus Andronicus: *A Retelling in Prose*
William Shakespeare's Troilus and Cressida: *A Retelling in Prose*
William Shakespeare's Twelfth Night: *A Retelling in Prose*
William Shakespeare's The Two Gentlemen of Verona: *A Retelling in Prose*
William Shakespeare's The Two Noble Kinsmen: *A Retelling in Prose*
William Shakespeare's The Winter's Tale: *A Retelling in Prose*